the colour of milk

the colour of milk

NELL LEYSHON

FIG TREE
an imprint of
PENGUIN BOOKS

FIG TREE

Published by the Penguin Group
Penguin Books Ltd, 80 Strand, London WC2R ORL, England
Penguin Group (USA) Inc., 375 Hudson Street, New York, New York 10014, USA
Penguin Group (Canada), 90 Eglinton Avenue East, Suite 700, Toronto, Ontario, Canada M4P 2Y3
(a division of Pearson Penguin Canada Inc.)
Penguin Ireland, 25 St Stephen's Green, Dublin 2, Ireland (a division of Penguin Books Ltd)
Penguin Group (Australia), 250 Camberwell Road, Camberwell, Victoria 3124, Australia
(a division of Pearson Australia Group Pty Ltd)
Penguin Books India Pvt Ltd, 11 Community Centre, Panchsheel Park, New Delhi – 110 017, India
Penguin Group (NZ), 67 Apollo Drive, Rosedale, Auckland 0632, New Zealand
(a division of Pearson New Zealand Ltd)
Penguin Books (South Africa) (Pty) Ltd, Block D, Rosebank Office Park,
181 Jan Smuts Avenue, Parktown North, Gauteng 2193, South Africa

Penguin Books Ltd, Registered Offices: 80 Strand, London WC2R ORL, England

www.penguin.com

First published 2012
001

Set in 11.75/14 pt Dante MT Std
Typeset by Jouve (UK), Milton Keynes
Printed in Great Britain by Clays Ltd, St Ives plc

A CIP catalogue record for this book is available from the British Library

ISBN: 978-1-905-49094-3

www.greenpenguin.co.uk

MIX
Paper from
responsible sources
FSC™ C018179

Penguin Books is committed to a sustainable
future for our business, our readers and our planet.
This book is made from Forest Stewardship
Council™ certified paper.

ALWAYS LEARNING   PEARSON

spring

this is my book and i am writing it by my own hand.

in this year of lord eighteen hundred and thirty one i am reached the age of fifteen and i am sitting by my window and i can see many things. i can see birds and they fill the sky with their cries. i can see the trees and i can see the leaves.

and each leaf has veins which run down it.

and the bark of each tree has cracks.

i am not very tall and my hair is the colour of milk.

my name is mary and i have learned to spell it. m. a. r. y. that is how you letter it.

i want to tell you what it is that happened but i must be ware not to rush at it like the heifers at the gate for if i do that i will get ahead of my self so quick that i will trip and fall and anyway you will want me to start where a person ought to.

and that is at the beginning.

the year was eighteen hundred and thirty by the years of our lord. and my father lived on a farm and he had four daughters of which i am the one who was born most recent of all.

also living in the house was a mother and a grandfather.

we were not within the habit of letting animals to live in the house though sometimes the small sheep would come in if they lost their mothers and we had to feed them in the night.

the story begins in the year of eighteen hundred and thirty. the years are of the lord.

the day it started was not a warm day to begin. no it was a cold day to begin and the frost was on every blade of grass. but then later the sun did come up and the frost went and then the birds were all starting up. and it was like the sun was in my legs for i got the feeling that i get. it goes in to my legs and then goes up in to my head.

the sap was rising up through the stems. and the leaves were unfurling. and the birds were putting a lining in their nests.

and the world was put in mind of spring.

i remember where i was that day for i was letting the hens out for they had been inside all morning for to lay their eggs and now they were to be let out for to run and eat worms and insects what would make the eggs taste and they was to eat some grass which was starting to grow after the winter that was so cold.

i opened the door of the house where the hens lived and the cock came out first and he was marching to music though there was none.

the hens stood in the doorway looking at the day and i did chase them out in to the home field and that is when i heard my sister beatrice calling out to me. she was stopped at the gate in to the home field and she was saying my name.

mary, she said. what you doing?

whatsit look like i'm doing? i asked.

looks like you been letting the hens out, she said.

really? i said. that's strange cos i ain't been doing that. i been dancing with the cockerel and then we had a feast together and the pig came and he sat on the top chair and he sang us all a song.

you don't get no better, she said.

how can i get better? i asked. if i ain't exactly ill.

you wanna do less talking and more working, she said.

and you wanna do less watching what everyone else is doing, i said, and do more of the doing yourself. so where is it you been?

at the church.

well that ain't gonna get the animals fed, is it?

it might make god provide their food.

look at me, i said, i been hauling round this big tub of food. i ain't seeing god doing that.

he might not be dragging the food round, she said, but he grows it.

well bugger me, i said, and i thought it was me who planted all that seed.

you shouldn't speak like that.

speak how i like, i said.

you'll get in to trouble one day.

will i?

yes, she said. you will.

i put my hands on my hips. i been getting in to trouble all my life, i said, but it ain't never stopped me saying what i think.

i noticed, she said.

so where you been did you say?

i been to church, she said, cos i done some cleaning cos it gets dusty.

i know it gets dusty, i said. i ain't stupid.

she tipped her head to the side. o, ain't you, mary?

no, i said. i am not stupid. and before you say it i ain't slow. i ain't none of them things.

beatrice walked off to the house and i followed her and we went to the back door. only she didn't realize it but mother was standing right there with the pail full to the brim of milk in her hand. and she was looking at beatrice with a look what says what you doing in the house? get out to work.

and beatrice stood there with her mouth open then she said to mother all sweet like milk wouldn't curdle, mary said i should come in. she said you asked for me.

and then beatrice turned to me and give me one of they looks what says you better shut up.

mother stared at her, then she said, get out. go on.

and beatrice went.

so that left me and mother in the kitchen.

mother said to me, so you done the hens?

course i have, i said. you asked me to do them so i done them.

so how many eggs?

eggs? i said. eggs?

she stared at me.

now, no fly ain't never rested on mother since the year seventeen hundred and ninety two when she was a week old and a fly come in the room and rested on her crib. but even then she was as quick as a river and she swatted that fly off her and from that day on they knew not to come near her.

yeh, eggs, she said. how many were there?

i lost count, i said.

lost count? how?

how? i said.

yes. how.

ah, i said, i know what happened.

she looked right at me. and waited.

i reckon, i said, i was so busy counting my steps coming back here it made me clean forget i was sposed to be carrying the eggs.

if you got time to count steps, she said, then you ain't got enough jobs and you'll be looking for more, won't you?

i nodded.

or your father'll have summat to say to you. and he'll have summat to say to me. so you better go get them.

and so i went back in to the hen house and i put the eggs in the basket. some was still warm and some had shit and feathers on them.

and one was under a hen and i pushed her off it.

i counted them all. twenty and that is not lucky for the eggs should always be odd so i put the one back under the hen and it was nineteen. i told them for to lay more tomorrow or they would be in the pot.

mother was standing by the table. and she had a mixing bowl clutched to her like as if she was stopping it from jumping right out of her hand and down on to the flagstones.

8

i put the basket of eggs on the side and went to go next door.

where you reckon you're going? she asked.

in to see grandfather.

don't you reckon you're staying in there all day. you wanna be doing less talking and more working.

i know, i said.

and i do know. but i can't help it. cos i am how i am. my tongue goes fast as the cat's tongue when he laps up the milk from the bucket.

i went on in the other room and there he was sat by the fire. there wasn't no flames. i sat in the other chair face to face with him and my grandfather looked at me and he smiled.

what you been doing? i asked.

this and that, he said, and some more of that.

i moved my chair closer in to him. did violet wash you?

o yeh, he said. she washed me all right. bloody scrubbed at me skin till it was nearly all rubbed off. she reckons i'm a cow she's getting ready for the market. mind, don't reckon they'd get a lot for me. not a lot of meat on me, is there?

i laughed and pulled straight the coat which was over his legs to keep them warm cos they were dead where he fell off the hayrick.

how many eggs today then, young miss? he asked.

not enough.

bugger. they'll be for it.

i'll be for it.

take them out some scraps. feed them up a bit. get a bit of fat on them. that'll get them laying.

pig has the scraps.

steal some from the pig.

9

i nodded. i will, but he's a greedy bugger.

grandfather wagged his finger. none of that language from a young'n like you, he said. mind, you speak right, he is a greedy bugger.

i laughed. so, i said, what you gonna do now?

not a lot *to* do. i'll have my dinner when it's ready. i'll have a bit of old shut eye after that. then i'll shuffle through and peel some taters, eat summat at the table with you lot, and then get on to bed and find meself another day nearer death.

don't say that.

why the bloody hell not? he asked. roll on death the working man's friend.

don't say that neither.

that what you come for, tell me what i can and can't say?

no, i said. come in to see you was all right. if you need anything.

all i need's two new legs.

o, i said.

yeh, o.

he looked at the empty fireplace then back at me. look at us, he said, what a bloody pair we are. four legs between us, and only one's any good.

we laughed and i stood up.

where you going? he asked.

she said i wasn't to talk all day. spec there's some jobs for me to do.

bugger the jobs. get your cheeks back on the chair.

so i sat down. you seen beatrice? i asked.

grandfather yawned. she's been in here, he said, boring me nearer to my maker than i was. praying for my soul she was, so loud she near made me deaf. what does she reckon? if she asks her god loud enough to heal me, i'll be jumping up from the chair and dancing? gonna need more than a miracle for that.

and he laughed. then his eyes started cos he laughed so much and he got out his thick red and white hanky and wiped.

you sisters, he said. couldn't get more different if you covered every woman in the parish, had a daughter out of each one.

but i'm your favourite, ain't i? i asked.

he stared at me, then smiled and nodded. course you are. but don't you tell one of they buggers i said so.

then we heard mother's voice outside the door. she still in there talking? she asked.

i stood up. i ain't waiting for her to come and thicken up my ear, i said.

i tucked the coat back round his legs and opened the window. i climbed clean out and jumped down in to the home field. shut the window behind me.

i went on round the home field towards the hen house and the other gate and i had a stick in my hand and i was hitting at the dead thistles and spraying their seed in the air.

what you doing?

i looked up and saw father standing at the gate.

look at you, he said, flouncing round like you ain't got nothing better to do.

i ain't flouncing, i said. i was only wanting to know where violet was.

she's where she ought to be, in the three acre. where you ought to be.

all right, i said. i'm going there.

then get on with it. ain't like you're special. just cos of that.

he pointed at my leg.

i didn't say i was special, i said.

i went on through the home field and past the hens and over the gate and up the lane towards the three acre.

i didn't say i was special.

and i never have said that.

and i never even thought that.

my leg is my leg and i ain't never known another leg. it's the way i always been and the way i always walked. mother says it was like that when i come out in to the world. i was some scrap of a thing with hair like milk and i was born later than they thought and for that reason i was covered in some hair like i was an animal and my nails was long. and she says i took one look around me and i opened my mouth and i yelled and some say i ain't never shut it since.

and some say mother was sick that summer and she was still working in the fields and she had this lump which was me and she couldn't very well bend down cos i was in the way.

and they say that my leg was twisted round underneath me and it ain't never been right since.

when i was a baby they tied it to some piece of wood to straighten it only it rubbed and there was blood and i screamed till they took it off and let my leg go in the way it wanted to.

and so that is the way i am.

i got in to the three acre and my sisters were there the three of them. there was beatrice and there was violet and there was hope. and i took my bucket and i started doing the same as they was doing which was bending down and picking up stones and putting them in the buckets till they was full then going to the cart to tip them in.

and as i was working the sun was shining and for the first time since the winter i could feel it on my back and the birds felt it too cos they started making a racket and it was so loud i could hardly hear the sound of the stones hitting the metal buckets and then i thought o well father might be like he is but here we are on a day like this and how can i hang on to being that cross. and then i started to feel it again where the sun is in my legs and it crawls up and goes in to my body and then it comes out in my head.

that night i thought i was gonna sleep like as if i was dead cos i was tired and my leg was aching but i no sooner dropped off as i was awake again and my eyes was open and i could not sleep.

the moon was bright and came in the room and for that i could see.

beatrice lay next to me and though she was asleep she still held her bible in one hand. i could hear her breathing. in and out.

most of the time in bed she has the bible in her hands and sometimes she opens it and turns the pages and she moves her head and her eyes from side to side only she can't read.

that is because father needs us here on the farm to do the work and he can not afford for us to be away at a school learning things which we would not be able to use for who needs to learn to read words and write them down when they are picking up stones from the earth and putting them in buckets. and taking milk from the cows and putting it in buckets.

beatrice stopped breathing and then made a loud sigh and she turned in the bed and her hand opened and her bible slipped out and banged down on to the wooden floor. only she didn't wake up. i didn't wake up on account of that i was already awake.

i have shared beds with all my sisters at different times and they are all problems. beatrice has to hold the bible and when you are trying to sleep she prays. violet is very long in the bed and is always saying that her feet are cold for they do stick out of the end and when she bends to pick up stones or potatoes she says it hurts her back for she has further to bend. and she has sharp elbows. and hope is filthy of temper and she will do all she can to take the covers and make me cold and she says she does it in her sleep but i know she is awake and doing it for the on purpose of it.

so beatrice made a sigh and dropped her bible and i was awake. so i got out of the bed and picked up the bible and i made sure that the dead nettle which she had dried and made flat between the pages was in there. and i put it on the top of the bed again for i know that if she wakes and her hands are empty of it then she will feel the devil has a hold of her collar.

i went to the window and pulled aside the blanket that is nailed to the frame. the moon was out and was lighting up the outside bright enough for there to be shadows like there are in the day when the sun is out. the cow was lying down in the home field and i could see the black and white patterns in her coat. and i went from the window and i pulled on my skirt and put my shawl over my shoulders. and i went out of the room.

i went down the stairs so quiet for that i was careful my bad leg did not bang on the steps for if i woke up father he would not be happy with me. i put on my boots and went through the kitchen and then the scullery which stunk of the new cheese and it stunk of milk too for cheese is only hard milk and i went out of the door in to the night.

and outside was cold and i should have taken a blanket to put on my shoulders only it was too late. and i went through the yard and i climbed the gate and went in to the home field and there was a ground frost for in the light of the moon the grass was silver. and the cow watched me and she did not move for she is the house cow and for that she is used to people and i think she even likes it when she has company. and so i walked up to her and she let me kneel down by her and lean against her and she was warm and i should have stayed there. and i wish i did stay there but i never.

the house was a black shape in the night. i could see the roof and the chimneys of which there are two but we only ever use one. and i could see where the windows were though i could not see glass but black shapes like there were holes in the brick.

there was windows upstairs and i could see the one which was my bedroom where i had just been looking out from. then there was another window next to it what is where violet and hope sleep. and there is another window what is where father and mother sleep. and there is another room what has a window but i can't see it for it is at the front of the house and that is where my grandfather used to sleep only now he can't get up the stairs on account of his legs so he sleeps in the downstairs room where we keep the apples and that is why the house smells of apples and grandfather smells of apples.

i left the cow lying there in the dark and i went back round the side of the home field and past the sleeping hens and over the gate and in to the yard. i do not know where i did think i was going only that i was having a look.

the air was still cold and i was starting to think that i needed to go back in and get in to bed. but the next thing i saw was a person going round the side of the barn. i thought it was someone in the yard taking some hay what was ours and wasn't theirs so i thought i would follow and see who it was so i could tell father.

i walked round the back where the barn was open to the field and the moon lit it up and i was careful not to make any noise. i stood still and was quieter than the church when it is empty. then i saw there wasn't just one person. there was two.

i waited. then i could hear a man's voice.

do they know you're here? he asked.

no.

o, violet, he said. come here.

i stopped breathing and didn't dare move.

and then i saw her and then their mouths were touching and his arms were round her. i could hear my heart. and then his hands were on her skirt and he was pulling it up and then he pushed her down on to the hay and they were lying down and he pulled up her skirt more and i could see her legs which were white and his hand was moving up her leg and under her skirt and he said o, violet again.

and he was making a noise like a calf when it looks for the teat and then she said summat.

o no, she said. you can't do that.

i can, he said.

and his mouth was on hers and then he was pulling down her bodice and she never takes it off not even when she is in the bed. and i could see the soft parts of her.

he pulled her legs apart and they were o so white in the dark night and he climbed on her and started to move and that is when i closed my eyes. and after not a long time the noises stopped and i heard him speak.

violet, he said.

i opened my eyes and i saw him kiss her and then she pulled on her bodice and pulled down her skirt. and he took some hay out from her hair and she said she had to go.

and so she kissed him and i stepped back in to the deep shadows and she left the barn and walked back through the yard.

and he stayed there a while then he pulled his clothes in to order and brushed himself down to get rid of the hay and then he left the barn and i watched him go out of the yard and walk up the lane.

i went back across the yard and over the gate in to the home field. the cow was still lying there. i sat on the cold ground by her and leaned back in to her flank and i could smell her milk and the shit on her tail.

i sat there and waited for my heart to slow down. and the grass was hard and silver with the frost.

i lifted up my skirt and looked down at my legs lying there on the grass. they was white in the light of the moon. i put my hand down and touched my own skin and then pushed my skirt back down and pulled my legs up to my chin.

i sat there a while with my arms wrapped tight around me, till i got so cold my teeth were talking to their selves so i got up and went back in to the house.

there is summat you must know.

i write this with my own hand in this year of the lord eighteen hundred and thirty one and i am proud that it is with my own hand i write it.

you will see why.

i told my self i would tell you everything that happened. i said i would say it all but i ain't done that. i ain't been true.

you see when i sat on the ground by the cow and i lifted my skirt and looked down at my legs lying there in the grass, i put my hand down there and i touched me in that place.

next morning beatrice had to shake me to get me up and it was still dark and it was cold and i pulled on my skirts and shawl and went down the stairs and out to the cows. i hollered them in and got the stool and lined up the tin bucket. the house cow was my first but then she always is and i leaned my head in to her as i pulled and my hands were kept warm by the teats. and the milk came easy.

violet was next to me on her stool and she was yawning and it was then i remembered what happened in the night. but then i thought maybe it was a dream and maybe it didn't happen but then she yawned again and i knew it was true.

and the milk hit the side of the tin buckets.

violet, i said. did you sleep well?

she stopped milking and looked round at me. why d'you ask?

i shrugged. wondered, i said.

well wonder summat else.

i carried on milking but i couldn't hear nothing going in to her bucket. i turned round again and she was still looking at me.

fingers not working? i asked.

brain not working? she asked.

i hit my self on the head. seems to be working fine, i said.

violet stood up and moved her stool to the other side of her cow so she couldn't see me and i leaned on in and pulled

harder on the teats and tried to think only of that and not
how she'd lain there in the hay and he'd pulled her skirt up
and the look of her legs pale in the light of the moon.

that same day the sheep needed moving up to the field by the
church what is called church field so i was told to go and help.
   hope was the one what went ahead and shut the gates
so the sheep didn't go in the gardens. i was the one what followed behind and opened all the gates what we had just shut.
it's better to be the one what goes first and shuts gates cos
when you follow you have to walk in the shit.
   we went along the lane and up in to the village. we went
past all the houses and hope opened the gate in to the church
field and stood there to send them through. and the sheep
went in. and we closed the gate in to the field.
   we stood by the gate and from there we could see the
church and we could see the roof of the church house what
is called the vicarage and then we saw him come out and he
stood and looked at us. he is the son what lives there and is
called ralph.
   he came to ask us if violet was with us. and we said no she
was down doing more of the stones in the three acre and we
had to get back to do it. then i asked why he wanted to see
her.
   ralph shrugged. because i do.
   you been down to see her? i asked.
   not with your father there, he said. i know better than that.
   so you didn't go down there last night?
   what are you talking about? he asked. he was staring at me
and i could see hope was staring at me and all.
   yes, hope said, what are you talking about?
   nothing, i said.

she's like that, hope said to ralph. she don't know nothing.

what are you doing? ralph asked.

we brought the sheep up, hope said.

i guessed that, ralph said. he was looking at the lane and pointing at the shit.

hope laughed. she tucked her hair behind her ear and smiled.

come on, hope, i said. father'll be watching for us.

don't listen to her, hope said. where you going now?

don't know, ralph said. it depends upon where you're going. what's your name? there are so many of you girls.

hope, hope said.

hope, ralph said slowly.

i pulled on hope's elbow and she pushed me away. go home, she said.

what about father? i asked.

tell him i'm sorting one of the sheep.

he won't believe me, i said.

she never stops, hope said. drives me mad.

she turned to me and grabbed my arm. she pinched me. hard.

get back home, she said.

ow.

ow what? she pushed me and i staggered forward.

go on, she hissed. go home.

i walked back down the lane to the farm. past the ten acre and the three acre, then in the yard.

father stood by the pig. he watched me walk in. where's hope? he asked.

she stayed to sort out a sheep, i said.

and then even though i moved cos i knew what was coming he clipped the side of my head so fast and quick there wasn't nothing anyone could've done.

get out to the field, he said.

violet was out there and she was rubbing her back cos it hurt but that is what occurs when you are that tall. and beatrice was throwing each and every stone in to her bucket even though it was right in front of her for she liked the sound of the stone on the metal. she was singing a song what she'd heard while she was in church hoping for a glimpse of god.

the birds came down to see what we was doing but saw we wasn't planting seeds and they soon left.

my head hurt a bit where he hit me but i was in the sun and the sun was warm on my back and soon i forgot what father done and i forgot everything except being there in the sun and hearing the birds and we started to sing the three of us as we picked up the stones.

the sun began to go down and the dark arrived and it was hard to see the stones from the soil.

we tipped the last of them in to the cart then i went and got the horse and harnessed him and took the stones to the copse at the end of the field where they'd not get in the way of any plough.

and it was black dark when we all went in to the kitchen. the lamp was lit and mother was by the fire. and grandfather was sat at the table.

hello, grandfather, i said, you had a good day?

good day? mother asked. he's just been sat in that old chair like the lazy sod he is.

he ain't lazy, i said. he ain't got no choice but to sit there. ain't like his legs'd take him anywhere.

might as well be dead for the use he is, she said.

wish i were dead, grandfather said, having to listen to you going on like that.

well i'm glad you ain't dead, grandfather, i said. cos you keep us happy.

happiness never did no one any good, mother said.

where's father? violet asked. and where's hope? she wasn't out in the field.

yeh. we had to do her work, beatrice said.

and that's when they come in. father first, hauling hope behind him, and her squalling and going. he had her by the arm and he shoved her down on the bench. blood fell out her nose and down her face and on the table.

no need for that, grandfather said.

every need, father said. she ain't chasing young'ns round the parish. there's work for her here.

didn't you go off chasing their mother when you was courting? grandfather asked. you was sposed to be bringing in the hay and you was off all hours.

you may be my father, father said to him, but don't mean you can speak to me like that.

father got grandfather by the arms and pulled him out of his chair and out the kitchen and in to the other room.

stop him, i said to mother. stop him.

no, mother said. whose farm is it? who's the man?

next day was ploughing the three acre and first thing we did was plough in the last stook of the old harvest to bless the ground to make the seed grow stronger.

each morning i took the horse out to the field and

harnessed her to the plough. come dinner time i sat by the plough and ate bread and cheese and drank milk. then i took hold of the reins and clicked and we set off again. we went along the edge of the furrows. from sun up to sun down. right through each of the days.

late one evening and i went in to the apple room. grandfather was laid out in his bed what was between the boxes and i took one box and turned it up the other way and sat down.

what you doing? he asked.

i got to have a reason to come and see you?

course you ain't, he said. how is the world?

still the same shape, i said.

you still ploughing?

i showed him my hands. blistered to buggery, i said.

don't say that.

they hurt.

you'll be done soon, he said. you'll all be lying round watching the seeds grow.

can you see him letting us lie down? i asked.

he lets you sleep.

only cos we'll work better next day and cos it's dark and we can't see nothing.

grandfather laughed. he put out his hand and took one of the apples out of a wooden box and he bit in to it and then he threw it across the room and spat bits out.

bitter as buggery.

so you can say it but i can't, i said.

i'm old.

you ain't that old.

bloody feel it.

you want me to find you a sweet apple? i asked.

23

no. had enough of these apples.

i looked round. you ain't got nothing to do in here, i said. don't you ever get bored?

what d'you reckon?

must be a bit boring when we're out working.

your mother's always in and out. telling me i'm lazy.

you ever get unhappy? i asked.

not for long.

i don't neither, i said. sometimes i have to remind my self if i'm sad about summat. other wise i start being happy again.

we sat there quiet for a bit then grandfather asked if i knew what it was the next day.

i never know what day it is, i said.

easter sunday, he said.

then it's church.

better get up early before church, he said. get up the hill and see the day break from up there.

why'd i wanna do that? i asked.

cos then everything you want in the next year will come true.

everything?

everything.

i was scared to sleep cos if i woke late and the new day would've broke and i would've missed it.

and so i had to reckon when it was time to go and so i creeped out of bed and pulled on my dress and shawl. i started towards the door but then beatrice woke up and she said, what are you doing? you never lie still.

i said, i am going up the hill for to see the sun rise for it'll bring me luck and don't tell me to stay in bed for i have too

24

much energy and my legs jump if i lie still and then i have to do summat.

it's the middle of the night, she said.

but, i said, it is easter sunday so i got to.

then you'll have to be waiting for me, she said.

and so i did wait while she pulled on her skirt and got her shawl and we opened the door quietly. i reached out and felt for the banister to guide me down the stairs and she followed. when we were at the bottom of the stairs i heard a door open and we both stopped still and didn't breathe. i waited for father's voice to be calling out but i heard some feet coming out and i knew it was not father for he would be shouting at us by now and blood would be drawn. and so we waited and it was hope who came down and we whispered and told her where we were going and she went back for violet who creeped out also and we all four of us went down and pulled on our boots and got out of the door and walked through the yard and then we got up the lane far enough to know we were safe. and when we did we all started to laugh and jump for we knew we were doing bad but there was so many of us. and what could he do?

so we walked up the lane and turned up the path to the hill what was muddy and overgrown so the thorns catched on our skirts. and it was still dark though i could see some light pushing the clouds apart.

violet walked first as she always does cos her legs are so long and then beatrice followed her and then hope. i walked behind them all as i could not keep up but i did not mind as i could look about me and be with my own self and i could hear some night bird calling out which i thought was a night jar but then it did another sound and i knew it was an owl.

and then i heard something in one of the hedges and i thought it might be a rabbit or it might be a badger for they like the side of the hill and they make a right mess of it where they dig their setts.

i called out to my sisters to ask for them to slow down or even stand still and wait for me to catch up but they didn't answer and they had gone up so i carried on up the path and then climbed the gate to go through to the hill.

the sky was beginning to get lighter and i carried on though i was getting a bit tired where i was going fast as i could.

the three of them were already up the top and i went and stood by them. we looked over all the land around. which ever way you look you can see the view for there are no trees and there is nothing in the way and you can see the whole world.

and as i stood at the top and my sisters stood at the top and all of us were there the sky started to lift above us and the clouds got small and went and the sky got lighter and the stars went dull.

then the sun came up above the land and the new day had arrived.

i turned round and round and looked at the view. in front. behind. everywhere. and some birds flew by then circled up above us. they took it in turns to lead then drop back in behind.

violet was the first to sit down facing the east and the new sun. the others sat by her and i did too.

so if you could dream summat today and it'd come true, violet said, what would it be?

i lay right back and put my head down on the grass and the cold was on my neck and through my hair.

beatrice? violet said. you got to answer first.

beatrice drew in a breath and sighed.

come on, violet said.

anything?

anything.

it's got to be to meet the lord.

hope sat up. well that's a waste of a dream, she said, you'll meet him anyway when you get through the gates.

you said i could say anything i wanted, beatrice said, and that is what i want.

all right, violet said. hope? what about you?

i'd like a different life, hope said, where i'm the only one in a house and i got a bed to my self and it's warm all year round and i ain't never got to go out in the dark and stick my head in the side of a cow and i have hot water all day long and there's people what bring me food i wanna eat.

violet laughed. that all?

there's more, hope said. i want never to be hungry and never to be thirsty and never to be so tired i'm falling asleep as i'm walking along.

you better get yourself a rich husband, violet said, only what'd he do to curb your temper?

i ain't got a temper, hope said. it's just i get tired.

we all laughed at that then we watched two rabbits come out and look at us then run off. the sky opened some more and the sun inched up.

you know what i'd dream? violet said. i'd dream that i had a school where all the children came every day.

who'd be the teacher? beatrice asked.

me, violet said.

hope laughed. you couldn't teach, she said. you can't read nor write nor nothing.

shut up, violet said.

that's a stupid dream, hope said.

yours was stupid, violet said.

stop fighting, beatrice said. we better get back down. father'll be awake and looking for us all.

the three of them stood and brushed their skirts down. wrapped their shawls around them.

violet nudged me with her boot. come on, mary, she said.

i took in a deep breath and the fresh air went down in to my lungs. it felt new and different from the air down there.

violet called my name again but i just looked up at the sky above and watched the birds and the moving clouds.

come on, beatrice said. we got cows to milk.

she'll come down, hope said.

they started to run down the hill and i listened to the three of them. laughing. shouting. calling to each other.

i sat up and watched till i couldn't see them no more.

and then i lay back down on the new grass even though the cold had worked its way through my skirt. i watched as the sky changed its colours and the sun climbed upwards.

when i stood up i could see the farm and the shape of the house and the lane and the fields.

what was it i would dream if i could dream something and it would come true?

what was it i would say if anyone ever asked me?

i didn't know. i knew i had dreams but i didn't know what they were.

he was in the yard waiting for me. he didn't say nothing. i didn't say nothing. i walked towards the house and he watched me for a bit then he stepped forward and grabbed my arm. and he dragged me in to the house. and hope and violet was watching me. and he pulled me through the kitchen and mother stood by and i was shouting and she stood and watched me.

he dragged me up the stairs and he was pulling my arm and my hair to keep a grip. he kicked open the door to my room and kicked it shut when we was in.

i don't like to tell you all this.

i don't. but i remember that day and i know it was the day when things changed.

and i told my self i would tell you everything.

you know that.

i said that.

i don't know what he hit me with. i don't know how many times he hit me. i closed my eyes and let him do what he did.

he made noises. he kicked the bed. he kicked the door.

then it stopped. he threw me on to the bed and he left the room. i lay there. i held my hands to my face and waited.

the door opened and beatrice came in. she tried to pull my face round to look at her but i never wanted to. she took my hands away one by one and she got a damp cloth and she washed me. i couldn't open my eyes like normal but i could see her looking at me.

mary, she said. you all right?

i couldn't nod but i could speak. it was worth it, i said.

i am sitting by the window and i am writing this with my own hand and i have to write in the hours of sun for there is light and the moon does not give enough light for it is dark at night and when it is dark i can not write.

i remember that day and i know it was the day when everything changed.

29

summer

this is my book and i am writing it by my own hand.

in this year of lord eighteen hundred and thirty one i am still sitting by my window. the wind comes through the cracks in the frame.

i am tired from doing this and my wrist aches from doing this.

but i promised my self i would write the truth and the things that happened. i will do that.

and my hair is the colour of milk.

the crops was growing fast and the blossom come and went. and the early green leaves come. and the birds was out. and the air was warm and the weeds was growing so fast that when we cut them down it seemed like the next morning we was out there with the hoe again and it did rain but not too much. and when the rain stopped the sun was out and that is why the crops grew so high.

and there was a lot of grass.

and the horse and the cows and the pig had a lot to eat. and the horse got sore hooves for the grass was so rich.

and they said that it was the best year for growing some could remember.

i drew water from the well and took it in to where mother was in the scullery. and she told me to carry the cheese in to the kitchen where i put it on the table. and it was heavy. and she got the wire from the drawer. the wire has two wood handles on it and she gave it to me.

mind you cut it right, she said, for if you spoil that cheese there'll be trouble.

and so i lined up the cheese and lay the wire on it and got the two handles and put the wire at an angle and so it would cut in to the cheese. i pulled the wire tight and then down hard and slowly it went through the cloth and down in to the cheese.

and i pulled down until the cheese fell in two pieces. and

the inside was yellow and the smell was strong where it come out the middle of the cheese.

now cut it again, mother said. and i cut off a big slice. and we wrapped the rest in a cloth and put it away.

mother took the wire and sliced off a bit of the cheese and she give it to me and said the person what tastes a new cheese first will get a baby.

so i put it in my mouth and it was strong near enough to burn my tongue.

i waited till i swallowed then asked, how will i get a baby from that cheese?

you just will, she said.

but how?

you don't never stop asking and asking, she said.

i like to know things, i said.

she took the wire and did more slices.

mother, i asked, if i had a baby, would it have a leg like mine?

don't know, she said. you don't never know what you're gonna get. see what i got with you.

she turned away and wrapped up the pieces of cheese with hunks of bread.

hope and beatrice were with the hoes and working and at first i could not see father nor violet. but then as i got close i could see them at the side of the field. violet was sitting on the grass. and father was standing over her.

father turned round to me and asked me what i'd been doing and why i was so long.

i told him i'd been doing jobs and here i was bringing the food.

took your time, he said.

went fast as i could, i said.

well your fast ain't fast enough.

what's wrong with violet? i asked.

she's lazy.

i ain't lazy, violet said. i ain't well.

father took his bundle from me and he walked off and sat in the shade of a tree. beatrice and hope came over and it was all four of us sisters. and i gave them their bread and their cheese.

violet unwrapped her food then turned away and was sick in the grass.

dirty cow, hope said.

she can't help it, beatrice said.

we been doing all her work, hope said.

i passed violet the flagon of water and she wiped her face with it and then dried it on her skirt.

we got to finish today, hope said, or he'll be having us work by the moon.

i'll be all right, violet said. she lay down on the grass in the sun and closed her eyes.

have summat to eat, i said.

she shook her head. i can't.

that's when father called me over to him and told me to bring violet's food if she wasn't eating it.

so i went on over and passed him her bundle what he unwrapped and ate.

i stood there till he was done with the bread and cheese and he took the flagon off me and had a drink.

sit down, he said.

i sat down on the edge of the patch of shade what was made by the tree.

mr graham up the vicarage, he said, his wife ain't well. and so i told him you'd go up there and help them.

me?

don't be thick.

why'd they want me?

their housemaid's left and they can't get no other help. he said could i spare one of you.

and you said yes.

he's paying.

why me?

cos you ain't exactly doing the work of a man down here. trailing that behind you. he pointed at my leg.

when have i got to go?

tomorrow.

is it just for the day?

no.

so how long i got to go for?

till they don't need you no more.

o.

father drank more from the flagon and i watched him swallow and saw the lump on his neck move up and down.

am i to go up each day? i asked.

no.

i waited. he didn't say nothing for a bit.

you're to live in, he said.

father gave me the flagon. he stood up and picked up his hoe. the others saw him move and they all stood up and they walked off with their hoes and got to it.

now there's things you got to know.

i hadn't never slept in no bed but my bed i share with one of my sisters.

i hadn't never been far from the house no further than when we take the sheep up to the top field by the church.

grandfather was in his chair and i went in and i sat in front of him.

there you are, he said, and he smiled. know what, mary? i'd give anything to be out in the sun working. i spent all them years moaning about the state of my back, now i'm moaning cos i ain't bent down looking at the soil. it's only when you can't do it no more that you miss it. mind, spose i ain't never known nothing else in life.

spose.

yeh. all they years just turning soil over then putting in the old seeds. Bringing up a calf then milking her. ain't never done nothing else. funny really.

yeh.

mary?

what?

what is it? ain't got nothin to say? devil got a hold of your tongue and pushed it back down your throat?

father told me i'm going up the vicarage.

i know.

how d'you know?

he told me this morning.

you never said nothing.

i said it now.

tomorrow i got to go.

he told me. but you'll be back.

but he said i got to sleep there. said i'm to live in.

you'll be away from him.

but i'll be away from you.

that what's eating you?

yeh.

thought you'd be glad to be shut of an old man.

glad to get shut of father. not any of you. not you. not the farm.

you'll be all right, he said. they'll look after you there. and you ain't gonna be no more than a half of a mile from us.

that night we ate in the kitchen late and went out again to do the last jobs before the dark come. grandfather sat out in the yard in his chair and he watched us cleaning out the barn which we was getting ready for to bring the new harvest in. the air smelled sweet from the warm and the pollen and it was full of dust from the hay we was clearing out. and we was all working together. and the birds swooped in low and ate on the wing. and the sun set red. and we all sang.

later we went on in to the house and we was sat in the kitchen and mother give us some bread and the window was open with the warm air and the moths come on in and started flying around the flame.

mother, i said, have i got to go?

you know what your father's gone and said, she said, and you know what he's like so fighting him ain't gonna get you much where.

and soon as she said that father come in to the room and no one said nothing else.

i went on up to the bedroom and laid out my things ready for the morning. skirt. under skirt. apron. stockings. shawl. i picked the dry mud out of my boots and put them by the bed. there wasn't nothing else to lay out.

beatrice came on in to the room. she picked up her bible and held it tight.

let's say a prayer for you, she said.

no.

come on.

she dropped to her knees and pulled me down with her. the floor was hard under me and she opened up her bible and looked at it like she was reading out only i knew she weren't.

lord, look after your child.

i ain't no child.

shush, mary. lord, look after your child and keep her well and content in her new home.

it ain't my new home. this is my home.

shush. thank you, lord. amen.

we climbed in to the bed and lay in the dark. i heard her breathing go quiet and slow and when it was steady i got back out of the bed and went to the window and looked out.

down in the home field the cow was by the gate with her black and white.

the year is our lord's of eighteen hundred and thirty one and i am fifteen years old and i think again of that evening when we was outside in the warm. where grandfather was on his chair and we was clearing out the hay and mother was helping and we all four girls was doing it. and the air was warm and smelled of summer and the farm.

and if i could stop time that is what i would do and i would stay in that minute for all my life and for ever.

but a minute can not last for ever.

i lay all night next to my sister upon the feather mattress. my mind was moving round startled like a new calf and i could not get it to settle. i tried to wonder what it would be like at the vicarage but i didn't know cos i wasn't there yet.

and i ain't gonna pretend i was all right.

i ain't gonna say i wasn't scared cos i was.

but i think i got some sleep.

i must have got some sleep cos i woke up.

and i was the first up and i laced my bodice and put on my skirt and boots and i got my stool and bucket and was the first to get to the house cow and as i leaned in to her and pushed my head against her i breathed in the smell of milk and shit.

and then when the bucket was full i let her back in to the home field and took the bucket of milk in to the scullery and covered it with a cloth then i went back in to the house and got my self bread and some apple scrape on it and i ate that with some tea which i drank quickly before i picked up my things what i had wrapped in my shawl. and then i went in to the apple room.

grandfather was stretched out in his bed between the boxes of apples and he looked at me as i walked in the room.

and i was gonna say summat but i heard father call my name.

i better go, i said.

go on then.

but i couldn't move.

you'll be all right? i asked.

grandfather laughed. course i bloody will. i lived all these years, ain't i? i ain't gonna be dying just cos you ain't here to keep me company. go on. get on with you.

the sun was on our backs as we walked and father walked faster than me and i was carrying my bundle and the sun was on our backs.

i ran to catch up only father didn't slow down. and so i was walking behind him and i could see his neck was red with the sun and there was lines on it with dirt in them.

father, i called out.

what?

slow down.

said i'd be up mid morning.

will i be able to come home and visit?

dunno.

will i be back for harvest?

father stopped. all i know, he said, is they gonna give me some money and you gonna stay there.

how long?

c'you shut up and get walking. they'll be waiting.

i followed him up past the church to the vicarage house. there was one door in front what was painted green with a brass knocker and letter box. and some flowers in the garden. and some windows which were big and were painted green same as the door. we went round the side and there was the vegetable patch and the garden and a man was there digging. and there was the back door. which was open.

father knocked with his hand and hollered and then a woman come. she was short and wide and wore a white apron and she had a small white hat on and she told us to stand there for that she would tell mr graham the vicar we was there.

it wasn't long before he come to the door. hello, he said and he and father shook hands though father's hands were filthy.

this is mary, father said.

mr graham smiled. welcome.

she'll be no trouble, father said.

i'm sure she won't. thank you for bringing her.

right better get back then, father said. he nodded at me and then was gone.

mr graham smiled. you'd better come in, mary.

we walked in to the house. then along the stone floor corridor and in to the kitchen where the woman with the white apron and the white hat was.

edna, this is mary. and mary, this is edna. you'll be helping her while my wife is ill. isn't that right, edna?

that's right, edna said.

show mary where she'll sleep, mr graham said, and she can put her things there.

i ain't got much, i said.

that's all right. edna will look after you, he said, and show you what's to be done.

and mr graham left the room and went off down the stone corridor.

edna looked at me up and down and walked round me. you a good girl? she asked.

yes.

you a clean girl?

try to be.

follow me.

we went along the stone corridor then up the stairs and then up the other stairs right under the roof where the ceiling sloped. there was a room with two beds in it.

you'll be in here with me, she said. that's yours.

she pointed at the bed over by the window and i put my bundle on it.

you got an apron?

i got this, i said, and i unwrapped my shawl and took out my apron.

it's filthy, she said. that all you got?

i nodded.

she looked at my shawl and my stockings and underskirt.

that all you brought?

all i got.

who've they given me this time, eh? come on.

we went back down the stairs and in to the kitchen. she opened the big cupboard and took out a white apron what she put on me and then she got me a small hat like hers and she pinned it to my hair.

let me see, she said. that's better though you'll be better again when you've had a scrub. right. spose i ought to show you what's what.

she closed the cupboard door and she started to show me all the drawers and shelves and said what things were where. then she showed me the scullery and the cold store.

and then we went in to the stone corridor and she stopped at the first door and opened it.

i could see a big table and six chairs. there was more wood cupboards. and there was a rug under the table. and on the walls there was some pictures of a woman and one of a dog.

this is the dining room, she said.

what happens in there?

edna laughed. what d'you reckon? that's where they eat.

then she took me to the next room only the door was closed.

this room, she said, is mr graham's study. that's where he likes to work and spends most of his days.

why you whispering? i asked.

cos he'll be in there now writing his sermon or summat.

she walked to the end of the corridor. this room, she said, is the drawing room. and she opened the door.

it was a bright, white room. there was windows all down one side which went from floor right up to ceiling. and there was the garden outside. and there was a wood piano. and there was a big rug with flowers and a table with two chairs and there was a blue bed thing what you sit on and on top of that there was lying a woman.

this is mrs graham, edna said. this is mary, madam. she's come up from the farm to help.

mrs lifted a hand then let it drop back by her side. hello, mary, she said. thank you so much for coming.

i didn't have no choice, mrs, i said. father told me i had to.

edna pushed me in the small of my back. i turned to her. what?

you can't say that.

why? i asked. it's the truth.

i'll train her up, mrs graham, edna said. don't worry.

i'm not worried, edna, she said. i'm sure she'll be fine.

edna pulled me towards the door. we got to go, she said. mrs graham is tired.

i'm fine, mrs said. why doesn't mary stay here and tidy me up.

i should show her what to do first, edna said. she needs to learn the proper way to do things.

she will with time, mrs said. leave her with me.

and so edna left. and i was stood there. i tried not to look round the room only i couldn't help my self for i hadn't never seen a room like it.

mrs lay on the bed thing what had a cover on it made of blue and there was the same blue hanging down both sides of the window and the rug on the floor what was thick under my feet had blue flowers on it same as the other blue.

mary?

yes.

are you all right?

i'm fine, mrs.

you look lost.

i ain't lost. i know where i am. it's just i ain't used to this.

you'll have to get used to it then. you are staying?

father said i got to. said your husband is paying for me to stay. says he needs an extra hand what with you being ill.

mrs smiled. that's what i was led to understand. will you put an extra pillow behind my head?

what's that?

what do you mean, what's that? you don't know what a pillow is?

no.

it's a cushion, only you have it under your head when you sleep.

we calls that a cushion, i said.

well it's a pillow. look, it's just there.

she pointed at a pile of them and i picked one up. she sat forward and i slipped the pillow behind her and she rested back against it.

her skin was white as my new apron. on her forehead she had a blue vein which was twitching like a chicken's leg after its neck is wrung.

they say you been ill, i said.

that's right.

what's wrong with you?

haven't you been told?

i ain't been told nothing only that i had to come up here and leave my home and i'm to stay till you don't want me no more and i'm to do what you say.

mrs smiled. my heart is weak, she said.

o.

very weak.

sounds like your voice is weak and all, i said.

she smiled again. i suppose it does, she said. my heart's

never been strong, but it seems to be getting worse. the doctor comes but there isn't anything he can do.

it make you feel ill?

i'm afraid so. a heart seems to be a pretty crucial organ in the body. it seems that with a bad heart, nothing else works. though i hope my mind still works.

sounds like it does, i said. sounds like there ain't nothing wrong with that.

she laughed a bit then closed her eyes and i was gonna walk away but she spoke. don't go, she said.

i stopped still.

you're from the farm. my husband told me.

that's right.

i've seen you and your sisters all before, when you've come to church. you really look like your mother now. although you smile a lot.

ain't hard to smile more than she does, i said.

doesn't she smile much?

no.

why?

she ain't got a lot to smile about.

o.

i looked around the room. where's the drawing? i asked.

what drawing?

edna said it was a drawing room.

mrs laughed.

you laughing at me? i asked.

no. it's sweet. a drawing room is where you sit. drawing room, morning room, sitting room, you can call it whatever you want. what do you call it at the farm?

i don't know. the other room, i spose. we got the kitchen and the other room and the apple room.

o. i see.

so, i said, what d'you want me to do now?

you can put the room straight. those books can be put away. she pointed at a pile on the floor and i picked them up.

where'd they go?

mrs pointed at the wall what was covered in them and they was all sizes and all colours. there, she said. where the gaps are. put them there.

i took them over and pushed them in and straightened them like the others. then i turned round. what shall i do now? i asked.

o dear, are you going to keep this up the whole time you're here?

i'm used to being busy.

then we shall have to find you things to do. what time is it?

i don't know.

the clock is there.

i don't read clocks, mrs.

you never learned?

ain't much use for them down there.

then how on earth do you know what time it is?

we get up when it's light, go to bed when it's dark. animals don't have clocks and they seem to manage.

i see. and when do you eat?

when your guts rumbles so loud you ain't got no choice. either that or when mother calls you in and says grub's up.

mrs laughed.

you laughing at me? i asked.

no. i like the way you speak.

well that's a relief cos i ain't about to change.

i must say you don't seem the kind of girl who's going to change.

i spose it's good you understood summat about me, i said, and i picked up the tray with a tea pot on and a cup.

looks like this ought to be back in the kitchen, i said.

thank you. i do hope you'll be all right here, mary.

i'll survive.

how old are you?

fourteen. near fifteen.

and when's your birthday?

later in the summer. mother was out in the fields and they say she was sweating. and it was when the barley was done.

and that's how you tell?

only way i know. so i'll take the tray on then.

yes. off you go.

i left the room and i went down the stone corridor to find my way back to the kitchen. only i went through the wrong door and i was in another room with wood on the walls and a big table with leather on it. mr graham was sat at the table. he held a pen in his hand and he was smoking a pipe.

hello, mary, he said. are you lost?

reckon.

that way to the kitchen. the door's beyond the stairs. on the right.

right, i said, and went to go then i turned back to him. mr graham?

yes.

are you gonna give me food or have i got to get it somewhere else?

he laughed. of course we'll give you food. you get full board here.

i stared at him.

full board, he said, meaning all meals and a bed.

you ain't gonna make me sit at that table in there?

50

no, he said. you'll eat with edna in the kitchen. and remember, the kitchen's beyond the stairs. the last door.

on the right.

yes. on the right.

that same day i was going along the stone corridor and there was someone else there walking towards me.

hello, who have we got here, then? he said.

me.

he laughed. i know it's you.

and i know who you are, i said.

and i did.

i knew one of you girls was coming, ralph said, only i didn't know which one.

well you do now, i said.

i pushed to go past him and he put his arm out.

not so quick.

i got to do summat.

you haven't.

i pointed up the stairs. look, i said. what's that up there?

he looked up and i ducked under his arm and i ran down the corridor in to the kitchen. i slowed right down when i got to the door.

edna, i said, can i help?

next thing was he came to the kitchen door but all he could see was me helping edna put the tops on the pies.

the evening was warm and i went outside the back door in to the garden and i sat down. i can not say i was happy for all i did think about was the farm and the evening before and us all helping in the yard. but i am not the kind of person to sit and mope and so for that i stood up and i did walk to the end of the garden and i did look at the cage full of fruit and i did take one straw berry and ate it and then i did look at the vegetables what were all in lines and there were beans and peas and there was a fork left standing in the soil. and there was a shed with pots in and trays of soil. and here was a house made of glass what had things growing in it.

and i sat on the grass. and it was not cold.

and the birds were settling in the trees.

and i was tired for i had not slept the night before when i was at home.

and it was getting slowly dark.

i stood up and went in to the house and in to the kitchen for to get a candle and then i went along the stone corridor and up the stairs and up again until i was in the room under the eaves.

the window was covered in white cotton and i put my candle by the bed on the box and i took off my skirt and i got in to the bed but it was empty.

i never did think i would say it but i wanted for beatrice to be there.

even if she was lying with the bible in her hand.

i had never been in a bed on my own.

and the bed was small and hard and it felt like i would roll out on to the floor.

i lay still.

edna come in the room not long after me and she put her candle down on the box.

and there were two candles and the shadows made two of things and she said nothing but she took off her skirts and all her clothes. and she stood there in her own skin with her back to me and she was wide and like an apple and then she put on a white dress and she did get in to bed.

52

and we lay there and then she leaned out of bed and she did blow out her candle and then she did blow out my candle. and the room was dark. and though it was summer the bed was cold.

and edna's breathing started and it slowed and fell deeper and then i knew she was asleep.

and i did try to sleep and i was tired but my mind would not settle and i lay there and i could not sleep.

i got out of the bed and lifted the white sheet from the window and looked out.

the moon was thin.

i lay back down and crossed my hands over my chest. and then i started to think about the churchyard nearby and the graves and all the people what was down in the ground and their arms would be over their chests like mine.

and if you are in the grave the earth will fill your nose and mouth.

i sat up.

i was quiet and she didn't wake up.

i went out the room and down the stairs and down the stairs again. the flagstones were cold under my feet which was bare and i went past the kitchen and opened the door to outside. i went out in to the garden and walked around then i went out the gate and in to the churchyard.

what are you doing?

the voice come out of the dark and my heart jumped.

it's me, he said.

i know who it is, i said. you shouldn't do that. you could kill a girl of shock.

it wasn't me coming out at night in the dark, ralph said. i was just sitting here causing no harm to anyone.

what you doing in a graveyard? i asked.

looking for some company.

very funny, i said.

and what are you doing up at this hour? he asked. are you homesick?

no.

have you been away from home before?

ain't been nowhere.

so are you running away from us? are you off back to the farm in the dead of night?

wouldn't dare, i said. father'd be turning my guts in to garters no soon as look at me creeping in.

that's very true. how will they manage without you down there?

how they did before i was born.

ralph laughed. you have a sharp tongue.

i got a normal tongue, i said. i stuck it out and he laughed again. you keep laughing at me, i said.

you're amusing. so what are you doing out here?

couldn't sleep, i said.

ralph yawned and stared at me. you'd be quite pretty, he said, if not for your leg.

don't you be looking at me, i said. i know what you're like.

i'm handsome, he said. and witty.

you're after the girls, i said.

girls? me? i don't think so.

i saw you, i said. in our yard at night. with violet.

he laughed. i don't think you did.

i saw you. in the barn with her.

he shook his head. why on earth do you think i would do that? who would have thought that a little farm girl had an imagination like that.

ain't imagined.

no of course not, he said. he jumped down off the tomb. so you really believe *i* would go down to your farm and start courting a simple farm girl and hope to marry and live on a farm for ever, delivering calves and ploughing fields? what an extraordinary idea.

i know what i saw, i said.

and i know where i've been. now you'd better go back and get some sleep. i'm sure they have enough work lined up for you tomorrow.

and he walked off.

it was dark in the single bed.

and my feet were cold where i was out with no boots. i tried to sleep but it would not come to me. the night was not going to leave me.

i thought of beatrice and wondered was she cold in our bed.

my new bed did seem as big as the three acre field with only me in it.

next morning i was first up soon as the birds started and the sun was moving up and it was getting lighter. i pulled on my skirt and got down the stairs. i went in the kitchen and first i got the fire going then i swept up and started on the bread and mixed and kneaded it then put it to rise. and then i got the potatoes what was in the scullery and i started to peel them and put them in a pan of water and then i put the kettle on the fire for to boil and i put the bread in to the bread tins and covered them for that they would rise again before being baked.

and when that was done edna come down and she stood in the doorway and watched.

i picked up the kettle with the cloth and carried the hot water along the stone corridor and went in the study and i poured the hot water in to the bowl for the shaving and i went back to the kitchen and edna was still standing there.

you ain't cleaned out the fire in the drawing room yet, she said.

i done the bread first, i said, and the water for i heard the vicar moving about upstairs. i was gonna do the fire next.

i do the bread, she said.

well i done it, i said. i had time and there was no point in me standing scratching my self when i can get it done.

and edna reached out and hit me so quick and so hard i didn't know for a second what happened and thought i walked in to summat only it couldn't be that for i was standing still.

do what i tell you, she said.

i nodded.

go and do the fire and i'll be along to check you leaded the grate.

i went down the corridor and in to the white room and i kneeled down in front of the fire and started to clean it out.

i sat at the kitchen table and had a wooden plate with some bread and cheese. edna sat with me only neither of us was in no mood to talk and make friendly. so we never said nothing.

the clock ticked.

i ate what i ate then when i was done i said what do i do now and she said you got to go and make the bed for mrs. it needs changing.

don't she like that bed?

what you talking about? she said. you just got to put the clean sheets on.

don't know what a sheet is.

edna shook her head. what you put on the beds at home?

blanket, i said. and coats if it's cold.

sounds like you was brought up in a stable.

i wasn't. i lived in a house, i said.

edna laughed. you may call it a house. reckon it was a sty where you was brought up, and your mother and father were pigs.

you may work here, i said, and they may have said you can tell me what to do and you may reckon you can clip me round the ear but i ain't got to hear you speak like that.

i stamped out the kitchen and walked along to where mr graham was in his wood room. i knocked on his door and went on in and he was sat at his table with a pen and some paper. and he was bending over.

o. sorry, i said.

he looked up. it's all right, mary. i was just writing my sermon for sunday. what is it?

i had to come and see you, vicar, i said, for i have had enough and i wanna go home. i don't like it here. i never liked it from when i come and i never wanted to leave the farm anyway and if father wasn't getting the money for me being here then i would never have had to come.

have you finished? he asked.

no. yes.

he smiled. you do speak your mind.

i only got one mind to speak so i ain't got no choice, i said.

i suppose not, he said. though the rest of the world does not think in quite such a clear way. why don't you sit down?

i shook my head.

why not?

i don't like to.

all right. now what exactly is the matter? i did promise your father i'd look after you so if something's wrong you'll have to tell me.

there was a knock at the door. edna stuck her head round. sorry, mr graham, she said. mary, you're not to bring every problem here. mr graham's a busy man.

he ain't that busy, i said. he's just sat here.

mary, edna hissed.

mr graham smiled. she's all right. she's fine here, edna. leave her with me.

she's got jobs to do and you're busy.

i said you can leave her with me. thank you, edna.

edna went and closed the door behind her.

i know it's not what you're used to, being here, but you have to give it longer. you will get used to it.

i won't.

look, mary, mr graham said. my wife likes you. that's what i care about.

but i don't care about any of you.

mr graham laughed. what are we to do with you?

let me go home.

not that, no. i have to go out straight after breakfast so look after my wife well today. try and get her to eat something. her appetite's poor. o, and mary –

what?

i'll tell edna to sort you out some new clothes.

ain't nothing wrong with these.

they're the only ones you have, aren't they?

i only got one body to wear them.

but you could wash them occasionally. cleanliness, you will find, is next to godliness. you are god's servant as i am and i must rush for i don't like to be late.

where are you going?

he smiled. i didn't know i had to tell you my whereabouts. i am seeing a parishioner. happy now?

no.

now give it a chance here, and remember, look after my wife.

i got the white room ready for mrs for when she come downstairs. i laid the fire and i put the cushions straight and i opened a window for to air the room like what edna showed me.

and then i had to go in the kitchen only i was careful to stay clear of edna's hand. and she gave me a jug of hot water and told me to go up the stairs and see mrs for mrs asked for me to go and no one else.

i knocked on her door and she said come in and so i did.

i put the hot water down and went to the window and pulled the red cotton off the glass. i opened the window so the air could come in and she could hear the birds.

it's a summer day, mrs, i said. the sun's shining and i got the room ready for you down there so you can lie on the thing what you got what you lie on.

thank you, mary.

and i got hot water so you can wash your face.

yes, i can see.

so you gonna get up?

i'll need you to help me.

and so i did. i helped her wash and then i had to help her in to her clothes.

when she was done she lay back against the white cushions and she was pale as them. i went to the window and looked out. i could see up the hill behind the house and i thought of the farm the other side of it and the day when we were all laid down at the top of the hill and dreamed of what it was we all wanted. and who would say i would end up in this house and be doing this. and i didn't remember wishing for that.

downstairs i made sure mrs was settled and though it was warm outside the sun wasn't yet round that side of the house so i lit the fire and closed the windows.

mrs watched all the while but she didn't say nothing. her head was back on the pillow and her hands was by her sides and her arms looked like they was made of china like a clay pipe. and when i was all done i was gonna walk out the room only she called me back.

mary, she said. stay with me.

i got to help edna, mrs.

tell edna i said i want you here.

all right. but i'm gonna get you summat to eat.

i don't want food. sit down here. she pointed at the chair.

i don't like to sit down in the day, mrs. my legs got too much life in them for that.

don't you ever get tired?

if i am i go to sleep.

you make everything sound so simple.

it is, i said.

if only you were right. tell me, did my husband go out?

yes, i said. he says i am to look after you and make you eat for he says you do not eat much. he says your appetite is poor.

then you had better get me something to eat. and while you are in the kitchen tell edna i asked that you be allowed to stay with me.

★

and so i went and told edna and then she went out in to the garden to get some fruit for she was to make a steamed pudding and i made mrs her food. i got some bread and cut small pieces of cheese. and i lay them on a plate and put it all on a tray with a pot of tea and i took it to the white room. and i put it down on the table next to her.

that's your food, i said.

she looked at the plate. bread and cheese?

yes, i said.

is that what you eat on the farm?

we wouldn't have no cheese for breakfast. we'd be having bread and tea.

o, she said. she smiled. that is not what i normally have.

well i didn't know that, i said.

it's all right. i'll eat it, she said. you made it for me so i will eat it.

go on then.

but not now. i'm not hungry, she said. talk to me, mary. you cheer me up. tell me what your farm's like.

ain't gonna talk till you eat summat.

i told you i'm not hungry.

and i'm not in no desperate need to talk about anything.

i folded my arms and stood there. i didn't say nothing and the clock ticked and she started smiling.

and if i eat you'll talk to me?

i nodded.

she picked up a small bit of bread and ate it. i stepped closer. go on, i said, and she ate a bit more. when half the bread was gone and some of the cheese was gone i went and stood by her.

sit down, she said.

and so i did. i perched on the edge of the chair for it was

daytime and i didn't never sit down in the day and i started to talk.

all farms are the same, i said. so i don't know what there is to say. we got a house and some places where the animals sleep and there's mud and in the summer the fields is full of stuff what grows and what's got to be cut to dry in the sun.

i know you have sisters.

i got three.

and you never had any brothers?

father says he wishes there was but there ain't nothing he can do about that. he's stuck with us, he says, and none of us can work as much as a man and none of us has got the sense of a man.

mrs laughed. do you talk a lot when you are at home?

they say i talk too much, i said. mother says i come out talking.

what is she like? do you take after her?

she's always doing summat. making bread. cream. cheese to sell. she don't have much time for talk but she says i can help her long as i don't prattle on but then i can't stop my self so she just has to stand it. only there isn't just me prattling on cos father's father lives with us. and grandfather is a talker too and they say i get it from him.

what's he like?

well he's all right. he sleeps downstairs cos his legs is no good. and i go in to see him cos he can't move round much and he's on his own a bit.

i can tell from your voice you like him.

i can't hide nothing in my voice, mrs. least you know where you stand with me. don't reckon i could lie if i was ordered to.

that's a good quality.

depends whether you wanna hear what i got to say.

i suppose, yes.

i get in some terrible troubles with being like i am.

do you?

yes i do. can you lie?

i waited for her to say summat but she never. and i was about to go on talking some more but she'd gone quiet. her skin was white and her eyes like glass. you all right? i asked.

i'm a bit warm, she said. could you open the doors?

i went to the big doors what opened in to the garden and unlocked them and pushed them open. the fresh air come in and i stood there a while looking at the grass and the table out there and i could hear the birds.

i knew what time it was though i ain't never read no clock in my life. the milking would be done now and they'd be back in the house. grandfather would be eating his breakfast. if they remembered to get him from the apple room.

mary?

yes.

would you brush my hair? but i need you to be gentle. my scalp gets tender.

i stood behind her and started to brush. how's that?

perfect.

she smiled as i brushed and i thought she was falling asleep but then she spoke. don't stop. you do it so well.

i put the brush down on the table. i'll only carry on, i said, if you have a bit more to eat.

mrs laughed. all right. just a little.

she took a lump of cheese and held it up and looked at it then she put it in her mouth and ate it. happy now?

happier, i said.

she laughed. are all farm girls so cunning? she asked.

63

i dunno what you're saying, mrs.

it was time to cook the food and edna sent me out to get some vegetables. the man was in the garden and he stopped working and watched me walk up to him.

you harry? i asked.

he nodded but he didn't say nothing.

edna sent me to get potatoes and beans, i said.

he just looked at me.

you got ears? i asked.

he turned and walked off and then came back with a spade. he stuck it in the soil and turned it over and the potatoes was there. i bent down and picked them up.

they're early, i said. and your beans is early.

he still didn't say nothing.

you do the horse and that, i said. edna says you do everything round the place.

i picked up the last potato and stood up straight. glad i came out, i said. good to have a chat with someone. i walked over to the beans and looked through for the big ones. he passed me a basket and i started to pick.

don't take them all, he said.

i ain't gonna, i said.

first ones is only for the vicar and his wife.

really? i said. you surprise me. i thought first ones was gonna be for me. thought you'd grown them all specially for me cos you heard i was coming.

that night i went on up the stairs and got in to the bed under the roof. i lay there for a bit then edna come in.

she got in to bed but she never blowed out the candle. she lay there and then got out of bed again. she pulled out a box what she kept hidden under her bed. and lifted it up on to the mattress and opened it and she called me over. come and see, she said. come and see what i got.

she lifted the lid of the box and inside there was a blanket spread over the things. she took out the blanket and put it on the chair. then she took out the things in the box. one by one. she unfolded them and held them up for me to see. i made these, she said.

she passed me one.

what are they? i asked.

shrouds, she said. for to be buried in.

and she held them up. one by one. each of them was embroidered with small crosses. and the stitches was all perfect.

this one's for me, she said, and this one's for my husband only i ain't got one. and this for if i have a child that dies.

she held up the last one what was the size of a baby. and then she laid them all out on the bed.

i had another small one, she said, only i used that.

she put her hand in to the box and brought out a piece of paper what was folded. she unfolded it and inside there was a cutting of hair. and it was a curl. and where she held it up to the flame i could see it was blonde.

i had a baby, she said, only i was on my own when he was born and there was a cord around his neck. and he never breathed.

she folded the paper back up and put it in the box.

after he died, she said, i was sent here to work. and i been here ever since.

where did you live before? i asked.

over that way. two miles or so. i don't see them, she said.

how old are you? i asked.

thirty two.

you been here years.

that's right, she said. she folded up the shrouds and put them back in the box then laid the blanket over them. she put the lid down and put it back under the bed.

i get cold here, she said. and alone.

she put her hand out and touched my arm. her hand stayed there for a bit then she took it back.

i never meaned to hit you, she said.

it's all right.

i was scared you would show me up.

it don't matter, i said.

it does. i ought to be glad of the company.

she got in to her bed and i got in to mine and we lay there not moving and i said nothing and she said nothing and then i heard her start to cry and i put the pillow over my head.

a woman called at the door and edna told me to tell mr graham she was asking for the vicar. i went in to the dining room where he was sat finishing his breakfast. and he was sat at the table in his suit made of wool what was brown and he had a notebook and was writing in it and doing some drawings.

what are you drawing? i asked.

just some birds.

o.

i like to study birds. see how they nest, listen to their cries.

why?

he looked at me. because i find them interesting, he said.

o.

he put his knife and fork down on the plate.

you eaten as much, i said, as our pig does in a morning.

he smiled. mary, he said, allow me to give you some advice. don't compare your employer to a pig.

o, i said. i wasn't meaning to be rude. we all like our pig.

even so, in the hierarchy of life your employer should be above the pig.

he wiped his mouth with his napkin.

humans and animals, he said, are quite different.

ain't that different to me, i said. there's things they both do that's the same.

he put up his hand. enough, he said. i don't think we should continue this conversation.

right, i said. but there's summat else, sir.

what?

i just remembered why i come in. edna said to tell you there's a woman to see you, i said.

there's always someone to see me, he said. tell edna to show her in to my study.

she already has. the woman's there now.

right. well, she'll wait for me.

he watched me as i cleared away the plates and knives what was used and put them on the tray to go to the kitchen.

you don't look *un*happy, he said.

ah, but you didn't say i look happy, i said.

maybe. but you are doing really well here. my wife is eating and seems a lot more cheerful. edna seems to have settled down and says you are a real help. and all that means i can get on with my work and concentrate on the church and the parishioners. he rubbed his chin and closed his notebook.

is there anything we can do, he asked, to make you happier here?

no.

there must be something. don't be scared to ask.

i ain't scared of nothing, i said.

but is there anything at all you need?

i got food and summat to drink. i got a bed and clean clothes.

but i take it you would like to see your family?

why you asking questions when you know the answer to them?

he laughed. you are a sharp little thing.

knives is sharp, i said.

if they have been sharpened upon your tongue they would be. i can see why my wife likes you being here. look, she and i have spoken and thought you should have the morning off. go on, go back to the farm. it'll do you good.

i can go home? i started ripping off my apron.

slow down. i mean when you have finished clearing away, and just for the morning. you must be back after luncheon.

i will, i said.

tell edna to bring tea for the woman in my study. and send your father my regards.

i will.

my hand is hurting and so i stop.

i look out of the window.

it is raining as i write this. the water falls down the glass of my window and there is a mist and i can not see to the end of the fields.

i have to stop to blot the pages.

i shake my hand for it hurts where i am writing so fast.

my hair is the colour of milk.

i am mary.

m. a. r. y.

the sun was warm that day as i went over the hill and down the other side. the yard was empty and i went on in to the house through the scullery and past the pails of milk and the churns and the butter pats. i went on in to the kitchen what was empty. i walked through in to grandfather's room but he wasn't there neither.

i went across and opened the door in to the apple room. the boxes was piled high but between them there was the bed and on the bed there he was.

he must've heard me coming cos he was smiling. look who's here, he said. well bugger i, didn't expect to be seeing you today.

hello, grandfather.

what you doing here?

they let me come to see you all.

i sat down on the box by his bed. he looked thin and his cheeks was sinking in to his face like as if a bad swede does.

what you doing still in bed? i asked.

they all gone out to the ten acre. the lot of them's out there.

so why ain't you up?

they're busy. got a lot of work on.

they could've got you up before they went.

don't fuss on.

ain't fussing. come on.

i put my hands under his arms and got him up. i took him out the room and in to the other and then i got him on his chair.

you need a wash, i said.

had one yesterday.

yesterday? i said. more like last year. you stink.

i went and got some water from the kettle what was still warm and a rag and i washed him and found him his other long johns and trousers and shirt and put them on him.

you eaten? i asked.

ate yesterday.

your guts ain't gonna remember yesterday.

i went and got him bread and apple scrape. and i made him some tea.

i sat with him and watched him eat. he dipped the bread in the tea, sucked the crusts.

so you gonna tell me what it's like up there? he asked. they good to you?

don't care.

you would if they wasn't no good.

spose.

so? come on. what's it like?

i dunno, i said. ain't like here. they fuss on and it's all got to be done fancy ways.

that's fancy folk for you.

i stood up and walked to the window and looked out over the home field. where's the cow?

there somewhere.

can't see her.

mary, he said.

what?

there ain't been no changes just cos you gone.

i turned back to look at him. i wanna come home.

you ain't missing nothing.

i am.

what?

you.

you're a soft bugger.

i know. can't help it.

i looked out of the window again.

father out there? i asked.

yeh.

so he's still alive then?

he is.

shame.

grandfather started to laugh. you're a wicked one, you are. wicked.

they were all out there. father. mother. violet. beatrice. hope. i could see them right at the end of the ten acre so i walked round the edge so not to step on the crop. they was working together in a line yet it didn't look like they had hoes.

i got closer and could see they was digging up the black-thorn hedge between the ten acre and the five acre.

father turned and watched me till i got close.

what you done wrong? he asked.

ain't done nothing wrong, i said. he told me i could come back for the morning.

what for?

to see you all.

violet was staring. look at you, she said. it don't look like you.

it is me, i said.

your dress, beatrice said. that all new?

i nodded.

and why you got your hair like that? she asked.

i touched my hair. i got to for work.

those new boots? mother asked.

yeh.

i ain't got none like that, hope said.

you been all right? mother asked.

course she has, father said. you been working hard?

i have, i said. they say they're pleased.

71

better be, father said.

ain't right, hope said, look at her in them boots.

father clipped hope round the ear and she cried out. get to it, he said. ain't got time to be standing staring.

hope stood on the spade and started digging.

what you doing? i asked.

taking the hedge out, mother said.

why'd you wanna do that?

more growing room, father said. more money to be made. gonna get the machine in to thresh it this year.

thought you hated machines, i said.

i do.

then why you gonna get them in?

cos it's faster. faster than if you were sons and done it. and doing it fast means more money.

while you're busy making money, i said, grandfather was still in bed.

no one said nothing and it went silent for a minute while we waited for father to blow.

so, he said, his voice hard like the spade in his hands. reckon you come back to tell us how to do things?

she ain't telling you, mother said.

i ain't thick, father said.

anyway, beatrice took him tea, mother said.

i never.

so who did?

i did, i said. i took him tea and bread. i washed him. i changed him. you ain't been getting him up.

father hit out at me and caught the side of my head. that's enough, he said. carry on like that and you won't never be coming back again.

★

72

upstairs in my bedroom nothing had changed. the bible was on the floor by beatrice's side and the blanket was still on the window.

i lay down on the bed and felt my shape still there.

it was like i wasn't never gone away.

like nothing had happened.

i went round the home field and found the cow tucked out of sight by the hedge. i stroked her and then i got the bucket and stool and sat by her. i leaned hard in to her flanks and smelled her and then i got some milk out. and then violet come up to me.

she pointed at the bucket. she's already been milked.

i know. and i know it's gone milking time.

then what you doing?

nothing. i stopped and the cow wandered off.

we didn't say nothing for a bit then she said, you ever see ralph there? up at the house?

course i do, i said. he lives there so why you ask?

nothing, she said. only wondered.

you want me to give him a message?

why'd i want you to do that? course i don't. stupid thing to say.

she kicked the bucket and the small bit of milk poured on to the grass and sank down in to the soil.

she walked away.

i stayed there a bit but the sun was moving over the sky and my guts was starting to make a sound so i knew it was time to go back up there. i went in to see grandfather and told him i'd be going.

come back soon as you can, he said.

i will.

make sure they look after you right. tell them if they don't they'll have me to reckon with. an old man what can't walk. he laughed. go on, he said. get on then.

i went on out and said goodbye to mother and to my sisters what'd come in for some food. they was sat eating bread and cheese in the shade on the doorstep of the scullery. and then i walked through the yard. and i walked back up the lane. and i could feel them watching me and then i turned the corner and they could see me no more.

i was polishing the dining room when ralph come and stood in the doorway.

what d'you want? i asked.

you're the maid and i live here. do i have to explain what i want?

i know you want something. everyone always wants something.

do they? he come in to the room and leaned on the sideboard. your boots are muddy, he said. they're your new ones.

boots get muddy.

how was the farm?

still there.

and how are they managing without you? have the cows all lain down and died? have the crops wilted and the milk turned sour?

no.

were your family happy to see you?

i stared at him. what is it you want?

you were late back, he said. it was all the talk at luncheon.

i don't care.

that's very rebellious of you.

is it?

what did you do down there?

farm stuff.

you're so informative. so expansive.

i opened the tin of wax. i have a message for you, i said.

for me?

yes for you, i said. from violet. she says hello.

why ever would she do that?

i dunno, i said. maybe you can go away and think about it. i spec you'll come up with a reason why.

very funny.

he watched me as i put the wax on the wood of the table and rubbed it in.

talk to me, farm girl.

i ain't sposed to be no farm girl no more, i said.

you're a house girl.

that what i am now, is it?

yes. look at you.

i ain't no different, no matter what i wear. no matter how my hair's pinned. i ain't changing so don't think i am.

no airs and graces? are we not rubbing off on you?

no.

i started waxing the side cupboard and pushed him off it where he was leaning on the wood.

look after your mother when i was gone, did you? i asked. she eat anything?

no idea.

don't you care?

no.

that ain't nice.

you haven't lived with it for years, he said. all i've heard about all my life is her being ill.

that's cos she is ill.

she wouldn't know what to talk about if she was well.

she's very pale.

she would be. she hasn't been outside for a decade.

she's short of breath.

you're beginning to sound like a doctor.

i can tell she ain't well.

how are you making your diagnosis?

i looked after animals all my life. i know when they ain't well.

have you told her you care for her in the same way you cared for the cows? perhaps i should tell her. she'd be very amused.

no. don't. you mustn't.

he laughed. i shall.

don't you dare. if you do that i'll tell her you went down the farm to see violet.

will you?

yes.

i don't care if you do. it really doesn't worry me. in fact, i make it my aim not to worry about anything. life can either be a chore or a joy. i choose the latter.

do you?

yes. he pointed at the table. hadn't you better polish it?

i threw the cloth at him and he caught it, his hand moving quick as an adder. why don't you? i asked.

he threw the cloth back. i told you, he said. no chores. all joy.

mrs was asleep in the white room. i put a blanket on her legs and closed the window. i left the room and shut the door careful not to make a sound. ralph was up in his room and vicar was out. i looked in the kitchen but edna was asleep in her chair by the fire which she'd let go out on account of the heat outside. and i went up to the room under the eaves and took off my apron and dress and put back on my old dress from the farm what was in the drawer and i put on my old apron and i found my old boots and i put them on and i didn't care for that they may leave crumbs of dry mud where i walked through the house. and i creeped down the stairs and out in to the lane. i went up the hill.

from the top i could see down over the farmhouse and yard and could see the fields and the hay laying in rows waiting to be gathered in to ricks.

the pig lay in the shade of the trees.

the cows stood on the grass.

i never planned what to do it was just when i saw it all i started walking down there.

i had to.

i walked right down the lane and in to the yard and they were milking there. and then i saw father. and then he saw me.

what you doing? he asked.

i come back, i said.

who says you could come back?

i say.

he shook his head. i don't reckon you could.

i can't stay there. i want to come home.

you can't.

he took my arm and started pulling me out the yard. i cried out and all three of the sisters was on their stools and they looked up at me but no one did nothing. and mother came to the door of the scullery and she watched but she never done nothing.

father dragged me back up the lane and past the houses and the church. he dragged me to the vicarage house.

the back door was open and he saw edna in the kitchen lighting the fire.

where's mr graham?

edna saw me. i'll get him.

we waited out the back door in the sun and father's hand held my arm and he gripped me and it hurt.

mr graham appeared. is there a problem?

she came home but i told her she ain't staying there. i told her she's staying put here.

mr graham nodded. mary? were you running away? i did let you go down this morning.

i said nothing. father nudged me.

aren't you happy here? mr graham asked.

i said nothing.

she's well looked after, aren't you? she's just a bit spirited. a bit strong-willed.

a bit? father said.

i'll make sure, mr graham said, that she doesn't do it again.

you do that or i'll come and sort her out.

there won't be a need for that. mr graham took my arm and pulled me away from father. come on, mary, he said, edna needs a hand.

he pushed me in to the kitchen and i listened to the two men talking at the back door about how there wasn't no rain for the crops and how the milk yield was down then father left and i heard the door close and mr graham came in the kitchen.

mary? what on earth was all that about?

i shrugged.

bring me some tea through.

so i made him tea and took it in to the wooden room. and i put it on the table.

thank you. have a seat.

i perched on the edge of the chair like a hen on the nesting box when she's about to fly off.

i wanted to say thank you, he said.

for me running away?

no. for being so good with my wife. i know you're not quite settled here but you are doing very well and i promise you will have times when you can go home to visit, but you work here now. you understand? mary?

i understand what you're saying.

good. then you agree not to run away again?

i spose. i ain't got no choice, have i?

i don't think we need to put it like that. i think the best is if you settle down and get in to a routine. then you'll get used to it and before you know it, you'll be calling this home.

autumn

this is my book and i am writing it by my own hand.

it is the year of lord eighteen hundred and thirty one.

outside my window the sun is pale and the birds have fallen silent.

writing takes a long time. each word has to be lettered and spelled on to the page and when i am done i have to look at it again to see if i have chosen right.

and some days i have to stop for i have to think about what it is i have to say. and what it is i want to say. and why it is i am saying it.

and it takes longer for me to write about something that happened than it took for it to happen.

but i must write quick for i do not have much time.

the grass got long and it yellowed shadows got longer. hedges filled with berries and apples swelled on trees.

and when i went out the air was different for it was fresh and new and after the sun went down i could feel some cold.

and in the morning and evening the mist layered and made the hills soft and the air thick.

and edna filled the kitchen with jars and pans and we were busy with the fruit and getting it in to the jars. and harry dug up all the beetroot and carrots and onions and brought it to the back door and we laid it down in sand boxes and put it in the cold store and then we put the apples in the dark. and he sacked up the potatoes and we made sure the bags was tied and the light could not get in.

there was a lot to do only all the time i was working i was thinking of them on the farm what with the harvest in the field and they would have the apples to pick and the pears and this was the time when every light hour was spent bringing it in cos if you didn't then you would be stuck over the winter and the animals would starve and then the people would starve.

it was time to start on the jam and edna told me to go outside and to collect some more fruit from the cage at the top of the garden.

harry was by the fire outside and he was smoking his pipe. he watched me walk up towards him and i was carrying the big pan.

you look happy, i said.

he stared at me.

i said you look happy. must be to see me.

what d'you want?

i smiled. i'd like some damsons and some raspberries.

i'm smoking.

i know, i said. i can see.

then you'll have to wait.

and so i stood there while he smoked and the smoke mixed with the smell of the bonfire and the autumn air. and i listened to the wood on the fire and the licking of the flames. and the damp leaves sent up thick smoke and i heard him sucking his pipe and the clacking of the end of it between his teeth.

and then he was done and he walked off to the box he had on the ground and he picked it up and poured the damsons in to my pan and when it was full he stopped and some damsons fell on to the grass and i picked them up.

you know what, i said.

what?

you only live once, i said. you'll be dead soon and when you look back you'll realize you had a miserable life and you didn't need to.

and i thought he was gonna say summat but he never. he just stared at me and he sucked on his pipe and i turned upon my tail and walked back to the kitchen. and i took the damsons in and they had a sheen on them and the purple was near black like a bruise.

that evening i went in to see mrs and i sat by her feet. and i was rubbing them with lanolin what comes from sheep and i was doing that for her skin got dry.

look at your hands, she said. look at the colour.

i held them up. the skin was light brown on the palms and the fingers.

it's the walnuts, i said, for i had been peeling them and putting them to dry all afternoon. it'll wear off, i said.

i suppose so.

i carried on rubbing and she sighed loudly

what?

the nights are getting longer, she said.

i looked up at the window what was black like a mirror and i could see the room in it.

i stopped rubbing her foot.

don't stop, she said.

i got to see to the fire, i said.

she watched me as i closed the curtains and then i poked the logs and they fell down and i brushed up the ash what fell out and i took a log from the basket.

i don't know, she said, what we did before you came to us.

i spec you managed.

i don't think we were as happy.

the flames got hold and i put on the log and then another. and i stayed kneeling and watching the fire.

mary, mrs said.

what?

my father was not a nice man, she said.

i turned round to look at her.

he had no kindness, you see. i think i was permanently scared of him. i think that's why i was happy to get married.

maybe fathers think they have to be like that, i said.

maybe. yes. maybe.

i watched the flames touch the log and blacken the pale wood where it was split.

my father had a job in africa, she said, and i was born there. my mother and i came back when i was school age. my father said i didn't need an education but my mother wanted me to. she said i was clever.

and did you go to school?

she laughed. not school, no, she said. i had a governess. and then my father came back soon after and joined us in the village. that is how i met my husband. his father was the vicar. my husband was kind to me when we were growing up. sometimes that is all we need, a small piece of human kindness.

i turned back to the fire and put two more logs on and i went back to sit by her and i took her foot and rubbed it.

that feels good, she said.

she watched me rubbing and didn't say nothing for a bit then she spoke.

my father's skin was cold when i touched him, she said, though i didn't touch him many times. he wanted sons, you see.

like my father.

yes. she smiled. like yours. i was his only child, she said, and i was a girl. i don't think he could have been more disappointed.

mine just wants people to work, i said. he needs extra hands to do the milking and bring the crops in and plough the fields.

and does he make you all work?

i laughed. you ain't got no choice, mrs. that's just the way it is.

is it harder work than here?

a lot harder. when i first come here i was looking for jobs for i ain't been used to it like this.

have you got used to it now?

i spose. though i ain't here through choice.

she smiled. i know that. you never let us forget.

i looked round the room. the rug on the floor was soft under me and the books were all colours in the candle light. the flames of the fire reached right up in to the chimney and i thought of the fire at the farm where father only lit it when the frost came and we shook with cold. and the flames never went so high for he never put too much wood on. he said that way the pig's heart what was stuck with pins and put in the chimney to keep the devil out was safe from burning.

mary?

sorry, mrs.

i was saying we married quickly. my husband proposed and we were married soon after. i had a daughter after a year but she died not long after she was born.

she moved her foot out of my hand and rested it on the bed.

that is when, she said, my husband decided to follow his own father in to the church. and then one year after he was ordained i had ralph. he is a perfect son.

there was a knock at the door and it opened. edna stood there.

excuse me, mrs graham, she said, only mary's sister is here and she would like a word with mary.

it's late, said mrs. but you had better go.

i jumped up and went down the stone corridor fast for i thought summat had to happen for her to come up to the house and i thought of grandfather and so i ran to the back door and violet was there.

what's happened? i asked.

violet looked past me in to the house and when i turned round to see what she was looking at i could see edna was standing there listening.

and violet asked if we could go off for she wanted to talk to me and edna said i could only it was dark and for that i was not to be long.

violet led me up the lane towards the hill. we stopped in a gateway and went through in to the long grass and the grass was damp and the air smelled of apples for that there were trees in the field and i tucked my shawl under me then we sat down.

how you been? she asked.

i don't care how i been, i said. who's ill? is it grandfather?

he's all right. no one's ill.

then why was you being as if someone was?

to get you out of there.

o, i said. well tell grandfather soon as i get a day off work i'm coming down. beatrice all right?

beatrice moved her bed in with us. she couldn't sleep on her own.

and hope?

bad tempered like normal. i say normal. i should say like father.

and mother?

she's all right. nothing ain't changed. except – and then violet pulled her shawl to the side and put her hand right over her belly. i'm in trouble, she said.

what trouble? i asked.

she took my hand and put it on her belly. it was tight and hard and then i felt something move under the skin. it drew right across like she had summat in there. i pulled my hand back.

it's a baby, she said.

o.

yes, o.

you told anyone?

no.

i know whose it is, i said.

she didn't say nothing.

it's ralph's, ain't it?

she nodded.

you told him?

she shook her head. i don't know what to do.

i don't neither.

so we sat there and we said nothing. the damp seeped through in to us and the night birds called out and the wind stirred the grass and the leaves above in the apple trees.

the moon was near full and lit up the edges of the clouds.

i dunno what to say, i said.

nor do i.

and so i stood up. i better go, i said.

she stood up too. you want me to walk you back?

no. i'm all right.

i started back towards the house and then i turned. violet was stood watching me. we looked at each other in the dark light and then she set off up the hill. halfway up she turned back and i turned back and we both saw each other but neither of us waved.

next day i was in the garden and i was gathering apples from the tree to take in to the kitchen and i had a basket and a long pole and i was poking them and then trying to catch them for if they land on the grass they can bruise and a bruised apple is not a good apple and it can make the others bad.

and as i was poking the apples and then catching them i saw ralph walk through the open windows of the house and across the grass towards me.

the next apple i missed and it landed on my head and he started to laugh.

i stared at him but he still laughed then i poked another apple and he caught it and put it in the basket.

i don't need help, i said.

i think you do.

i turned my back on him and got my next apple only he jumped forward and put his arm on me and caught it from under my nose.

i'm leaving soon, he said. will you miss me?

i'll never miss you, i said. where you going?

time to go up to oxford, he said.

what you doing there?

university. studying. getting myself an education.

i poked the stick and a few apples fell down and he caught two but others fell to the grass.

thought you was gonna catch them, i said.

i did.

you gotta catch them all. i was better when it was me doing it.

give me the stick.

and he started pulling down the branches and hanging on to them while i pulled the apples off.

when we filled the basket i went to take it in the kitchen like edna told me. you want me to carry it? ralph asked. he reached out and touched my hand.

don't go touching me, i said. i know what you're like.

he laughed. don't worry. i'm not going to do anything to you. you're safe with me.

my sister wasn't.

not that again. you can be boring for someone who's normally fun.

she's having a baby.

what? he said.

she is having a baby. her belly is fat.

very funny.

she came to see me yesterday. she said it's your baby.

you don't know what you're talking about.

i am a farm girl. i know what happens. she showed me and i could feel it moving.

if she is, it's nothing to do with me.

o, i said. that's strange cos that's not what she says.

girls will say anything.

not violet.

of course she will. they go off with strange men and then say stupid things like that.

but i heard you that night in the yard. and i saw you.

if it was night then it was dark and you wouldn't be able to see me. and, he said, even if it was all true i won't be here anyway. i'll be many miles away.

will you?

yes. o dear, come on now. don't look so serious.

and he took the basket from my hands and walked off.

i am stopping now for i need to lay down and rest.

there is much to tell for you need to know it all and then you will understand.

my arm aches.

my hand has the cramps.

if i close my eyes i can go back and remember everything.

we spent a whole day peeling apples and onions and weighing fruit and measuring vinegar before we cooked a vat of chutney so strong it caught our throats as it boiled and we had to open the doors and windows.

and i was given a pile of wheat straw and i sat with edna

and she taught me to weave it in to a doll and then some others in to wreaths and bells and hearts and horse shoes.

and i took the straw doll i liked the most in to mrs and showed her only she was lying there and she looked more pale even than normal and ralph was sitting with her on the chair. and i asked her if she was all right.

no, she said.

can i get you summat? i asked.

persuade my son not to go away.

i don't think even your precious mary could do that, ralph said. anyway, she'll get over the shock, won't you? he patted her hand.

i will miss you, mrs told him.

tell her she'll be all right, ralph said.

he's right, i said. you will be all right, mrs. i'll keep you company. you have me and everyone else here.

you see, ralph said. he stood up. i told you everything would be all right. stay with her, mary.

and then he was gone.

and we was there in the room with the ticking of the clock and the licking of the flames and the weak sun coming in through the big windows.

sit with me, mary.

only for a moment. i got jobs i got to do.

i stayed for a while then she rested back against the pillow and closed her eyes. her breathing got deep and slow and i let go of her hand and got up to go.

i stood at the door and looked back at her and she was pale and her breathing slow in the quiet room.

in the kitchen edna was making a pudding and mixing suet in to the flour. she told me to peel the potatoes and the carrots and so i did bring a colander and a pan of water to the table and started.

when's ralph's leaving? i asked.

tomorrow. i been packing his bags.

he was in with mrs, i said. she's sad but i don't know why. she don't know what he's really like. he don't care about nothing.

i put the first potato in the pan of water.

people never see the bad, i said, when it's that close to them. like the pig when she lies in her own shit.

you wanna watch your mouth.

why? i can say what i want.

you got a good job here.

ain't a job. i don't get paid. i just got told to come here and live here and work here instead of home.

your father gets paid for what you do.

but i don't.

you got a roof over you. got a bed. got your clothes. you get good food. edna picked up the rolling pin and waved it at me. you wanna be watching it.

what do i wanna watch? i asked. that pin? you ain't gonna hit me with that. i reached out and took the pin from her, put it on the table. i ain't grateful, i said. i ain't never gonna be grateful for what i got here.

i told him you'd be trouble when he said you was coming, she said. i told him. i said you don't wanna be getting one of his girls. your father's temper's got to be in you all.

you shouldn't talk about him like that, i said.

why? you ain't gonna try and tell me he ain't like he is.

no, i said. but it's for me to say things about him. not you.

and then the door to the kitchen opened and mr graham came in. mary, he said. bring me a pot of tea to my study, please.

dunno why he asks you, edna said when he was gone. i used to take him his tea.

he wasn't sat in the chair where he normally sat. he was stood by the window looking out and he was wearing his suit and he saw me and rushed over to clear a space on his desk for me to put the tray.

and then he closed the door behind me and told me to sit down and i did.

ralph is leaving tomorrow, he said.

yes, i said. mrs told me.

i want to talk to you for i believe her health has been deteriorating for some time and i am concerned about what effect this may have upon her. i want you to spend time with her, keep an eye on her.

yes, sir.

i can rely upon you, can't i?

of course you can.

that's excellent. pour my tea, will you?

i put the milk in and balanced the strainer on the cup and poured. i passed him the cup and saucer and when i leaned forward to put it in his hands i saw his pen and an open book.

what's that? i asked.

what?

that book there, i said.

it's a note of all the birds that have come in to the garden.

o. why'd you wanna do that?

i don't know. no one's asked that before. i suppose i like to know which ones are returning year after year. keep a record of how they come and go with the seasons. i record their mating patterns and whether anything changes if there's a cold winter or a mild spring.

so you do that and the being a vicar?

yes.

and that's writing sermons and telling people what to do.

he smiled. that's not quite how i'd describe it, but i see what you mean.

don't seem much for a job.

maybe it doesn't to you. i suppose you were always surrounded by workers. i mean on the farm. people working all day.

if you don't work, i said, you don't eat.

of course.

why'd you do this?

what?

this being a vicar?

he put his hands together and looked out of the window.

i felt called to it. and, i suppose, i followed my father in to a profession. and then of course my wife's health was not good and so it seemed perfect for i would be able to come in and out of the house and look after her.

only i look after her, i said.

he stared at me. you really are outspoken.

am i, sir? i just think i say the truth.

perhaps.

only people don't want to hear it.

not always, no.

but i can't be no other way. cos that is what i am.

i stood up.

can i go now? i asked.

yes. but before you go. what do you know about birds?

me, sir?

he nodded. yes. you.

i know there's different ones and they come depending on

what crop we grow in what field. and i know there's some what stays in winter and some what goes and then comes back.

and do you know their names?

some, i said. father told us the ones what eat what we try and grow. he told us the ones what he wants to kill. the ones what you can eat if you ain't got nothing else.

would you like to know some of their names? he asked. i could teach you.

if that would make you happy, i said.

but would it make you happy? he asked.

i didn't know you was worried about what made me happy, sir.

he stared at me and then i was gone, closing the door behind me.

that night i went in to the white room for to tidy and lay the fire for the next morning. and it was late and mrs had gone on up to bed. the door was closed and i opened it and i went on in and i did have a candle and i knelt in front of the fire and the ashes were still too hot to clear and so i went back on my heels and i was looking at the ashes and thinking about the rabbit what was hung in the scullery and what edna was gonna make with it cos she said she might make a pie but then she might make a stew. and there was this voice behind me and it made me jump so hard i near enough fell in to the ashes.

mary?

i turned round quick and where my eyes was getting used to the light on the one candle i could see the shape of her lying down.

what you doing? i asked. i thought you was in bed.

i know. i couldn't rest so i came back down.

you need to rest, i said.

i can't.

i carried the candle over and put it on the table by her.

you want summat to eat or drink?

no.

you want me to do anything?

no.

i put a blanket over her and felt her hand. you're cold.

i can't feel it.

you are.

i got another blanket and put it on top.

why don't you go up to bed? i'll come and make you comfortable.

i'm not going anywhere.

i knelt down on the floor by her. then i ain't going nowhere.

we were there for a while. the air in the room was getting cooler and after a bit i went over to the fire and i put on some kindling and the heat lit it and then i put on some small logs until the fire was burning again.

thank you, mrs said.

that's all right.

i broke something, she said. i was trying to open the piano.

i carried the candle over and saw the broken china cup on the floor. i picked up the pieces.

i wanted to hear it, she said. i used to play a lot when i was young.

you want to hear it now? i asked.

can you play?

i laughed. no. where d'you reckon i'd learn to play? in the pig sty? in the hen house?

your life was very different there, wasn't it?

it was.

i wonder what will happen next to you.

i'll sleep and wake up and the bread'll be made. and i'll do the cleaning and all my jobs. there ain't nothing else gonna happen to me.

i opened the lid of the piano and even in the dark i could see the white keys and the small black ones. i pressed one down only there wasn't no sound.

press harder. quicker.

i pressed quickly and the sound came out.

it still sounds the same, she said.

you want to play it?

she shook her head. no.

i closed the lid.

come and sit here, she said.

i carried the candle over and i sat down on the rug. she reached her hand out and touched my hair and i didn't move but stayed there and then she stroked me like i was a cat.

i imagine your mother misses you, she said.

i don't reckon.

i'm sure she does.

her hand went still for a bit then started again.

you know, she said, it seems when you have a baby your whole life is that child and you never imagine that they will grow up and not need you and want to leave.

you can't stop them growing up, i said.

i know. but you can't imagine what it's like. you give up everything to look after them and keep them safe and then they leave. it's as though they have consumed you to gain their own life.

she put her hand on my shoulder and i put mine on top of it. you'll put me off having any, i said.

don't let me do that. she grabbed my wrist. don't let me.

i'm teasing you. if i want a child i'll have one. and if i don't i won't.

you shouldn't tease.

i know, i said, but i can't help my self.

and we sat there and the fire got stronger and we could feel the warm in the room and the clock ticked and an owl outside called for another owl.

o mary, she said, i don't want tomorrow and i don't want time to ever move forward.

the next morning i was carrying hot water to the vicar's study where he shaved before eating his breakfast. ralph stopped me in the stone corridor and put his arm across so i couldn't go forward.

so i'm leaving, he said.

i know.

while i'm gone, i hope you don't have any ideas of telling my father anything.

i don't know what you mean. what would i tell him?

you do. now listen. i insist you won't tell him anything and in return i won't tell him anything about you.

you ain't got nothing to tell him about me.

o yes i do, little farm girl. he grabbed my face and bent forward and kissed me and his lips touched my lips. i pushed him away and he started laughing. how dare you kiss me, he said.

i never.

how dare you.

i never. i never.

see. you don't want me telling him that you keep trying to kiss me and that you creep around the house at night waiting outside my door, making a chase for me.

i wouldn't do that. i wouldn't never.

wouldn't you? really? he stroked my face then walked away.

i never done none of that.

you know i never.

that same morning ralph carried his bags down and took them to the front door. he went back down the corridor and knocked on the vicar's study and i was watching this from the kitchen doorway. and the vicar came out and shook ralph's hand.

good luck, son, he said. work hard.

ralph patted his father on his arm. i will.

now go and say goodbye to your mother. be gentle.

we waited while he was in the white room then he came back out.

how was she? mr graham asked.

ralph shrugged. as you'd expect. he saw me further up the corridor and called out. where's edna?

upstairs, i said. she's got a day off. you want me to tell her to come down?

no. no need. you can say goodbye to her.

and then he walked past me. and his carriage was there and harry was loading all the bags and then the horses left.

edna was sat on her bed and i told her ralph was gone and that he said to say goodbye and she just nodded.

you going out? i asked. you got the day off. you could see your family.

they don't want me to come home, she said.

o.

i stood there and then she shook her head.

you sad he's gone?

ain't that, she said. i known him since he was born. looked after him all those years and he never said nothing.

i didn't know what to say so i left her and went down the stairs and in the white room to see mrs.

she was lying down and her head was turned away from me and i pulled up the chair and i sat by her and i never said nothing but waited for her to speak to me. only i sat there for a long time and she never moved. then i stood up and went and got her some tea and i got her to sit up and drink and then i lit the fire for her skin did feel cold to me.

and i did try to make her speak. i did try. but she wouldn't.

and so i sat there all day between doing my jobs and i sat there until the light did begin to go and then i went to help her up to go to bed only she said she couldn't.

leave me here, she said.

you have to go upstairs.

i won't go anywhere.

and so i went down the corridor and knocked on the door of the study and asked mr graham to come and talk to her and he followed me and he stood by her.

come on, he said. you have to go to bed.

but she said nothing. she turned her face away from us.

go and get her night things, he said, and so i went up to her room and found them and brought them back down.

mr graham stood by the fire.

make her comfortable for the night, he said, and then he left the room.

and so i undressed her much as i could and i put her a soft pillow and stretched her out and covered her with blankets and i stoked the fire and then i sat by her and blew out the candles. and the room was lit by the fire.

and i sat there for a long time and i knew she was asleep and then mr graham came back in the room.

you have to go to bed, he said, for i can look after her. and you do not need to.

and so i did. i went up the stairs with my candle and i went in to the room and got in to my bed under the eaves.

edna was already there and her bed creaked as she turned over. i waited and listened for to see if the breathing was slow but it wasn't. then i heard her get out of bed and she cupped the candle with her hand and the light was all over the walls and her shadow was big on to the ceiling.

i lay still as a cat in the sun and waited. and she opened the box from under her bed again and looked at the three shrouds then she folded them up and put them away and put the box back under the bed. then she blew out the flame and the room returned to black and i heard her bed creak again as she got in it.

next morning i got up and went down the stairs. i went in to the kitchen and got the fire burning and then i lit the fire in the study. and then i walked along the stone corridor and stood outside the white room. i listened but could hear nothing and i quietly opened the door.

she lay on the bed. her white arm with its blue veins dangled down and her hand brushed the floor. mrs, i said. mrs. i ran towards her. pulled her arm up and i kept saying it. mrs. mrs.

she opened her eyes only slowly and the blue was pale and i cupped her face right round in my hands.

can you hear me?

and i knew she could for her eyeballs went smaller.

i whispered at her. mrs. come on.

i lay her back down and told her to stay still and i ran for mr graham who was coming down the stairs and i told him to come with me. and he did.

the doctor came and left and i heard his horse on the lane. and i went back fast as i could for to go and stoke the fire and make the room warm. and then i made her some tea and went and sat by her.

you want me to tell you about my sisters? i asked. or the farm? you want me to talk to you?

but she never said nothing. i stroked her hair but didn't dare use the brush for if it hurt her. and i took the lanolin cream and i rubbed her hands. and i watched as she closed her eyes for a sleep and then i stayed and watched for her to wake up and she did only she didn't say nothing and mr graham come in the room and then i went.

and this is what happened for day after day. and then i took my bedding down the stairs and in to her room for that i could sleep by her and make sure she had what she needed. and edna did the cooking and that is how i became the nurse.

and on one morning mr graham came in the room and he said i should go and get some air and if i wanted to that i could go back to the farm for to see them all only i didn't like to leave mrs like that and i said no. i said i would stay instead. and so i did.

and so he sat by me on a chair and i sat on an other. and i said do you think you should tell ralph to come back and see her. but he said no. it wasn't necessary. ralph, he said, was now at university and was studying and was not to be disturbed.

but, i said, mrs would like him to come and see her.

i know, he said, but i have stated my opinion.

and we sat there until a bird landed on the window sill and mr graham pointed it out to me. what's that one? he asked.

that is the black one what eats grain, i said.

that is a crow. and do you know the difference between a crow and a raven and a jackdaw?

yes, i said. they got different names.

then he explained the difference between them all and how they eat and how they feed their young and how they live.

and then he said i should make some fresh tea and bring in some cake. and i did. and then he looked at the tray and he looked at me and then he told me to get another cup for me to drink with him.

so that is how it is that we sat side by side and drank tea together.

i don't know how many days i was washing her face and hands and changing her bedclothes and turning her to stop her getting sores. she didn't want to drink though i put tea to her lips.

but she never ate again.

and then one day i woke in the chair for i had told my self not to sleep but i did sleep. and when i woke she opened her eyes and looked at me and she smiled and then she closed her eyes.

i jumped to my feet and went to her. i listened but could hear nothing. i took her small mirror and put it by her mouth only there was no breath to steam it up. the mirror stayed silver.

*

my hand hurts again and my wrist hurts and i wish not to tell this.

i wish not to write it.

i wish not to read it.

and so the house fell silent.

and it was me who took off her clothes and lay her out flat and washed her. it was me put pennies on her eye lids. it was me made her white skin clean.

it was me what brushed her hair.

it was me what put on her clothes and pushed her heavy arms and legs in to a dress. i did put a ribbon in her hair.

and then the men come in the room and put her in the coffin and there was blue in it and they placed it on a table and there was chairs to sit with her.

and every day i went in to the white room and i did look at her.

and i did close the door and i did sit with her.

stop.

look up. out of the window. breathe.

after some days the sexton did dig a hole in the graveyard and mr graham did go in to his study and he did write with his pen and ink.

and with edna we was in the kitchen and we was making cakes and then we cleaned the house and then we went in to the church and we waxed the pews and scrubbed the floor.

and then the men lifted the coffin and ralph walked after and mr graham did talk about her and led the prayers.

and we were in the kitchen and the window was open and we could hear the singing.

and the women waited in the house. and the men went to church.

and the bells begun ringing.

and then the front door of the house opened and the men come in.

and the house was no longer silent. for it was full of people.

and they all ate the cakes and drunk the tea and then they all left. ralph and mr graham were in the study. me and edna cleaned the house and washed the plates and glasses and put them back in the cupboards.

the house fell silent again.

i went in to the white room. i closed the door behind me so i could be quiet. the windows were open where we were airing the room and the bed where she slept had gone. but the blue cushions were still there and i picked one up and held it. i looked round. there was the pile of writing paper and envelopes. a folder of letters she got. one book on the table. i picked it up and went to the bookshelf and put it away where i could see a space for it.

and then i went and stood by the open window and looked out at the garden. and the light was going.

i heard the door in to the room open behind me and i thought it would be edna come to close the windows.

mary.

i turned round to see ralph in his black suit.

i looked for you outside, he said. i thought you'd gone to the churchyard.

well i ain't, i said.

clearly i can see that. what are you doing in here?

come to tidy up, i said.

and what will you do now? he asked.

i don't know.

are you going back down the farm now your job is over?

i don't know, i said again. your father ain't told me yet what he wants me to do.

he'll probably tell you now. he's been busy with preparing all the funeral.

what are you gonna do?

i go back to university tomorrow.

what are you studying?

he smiled. i'd forgotten what you're like, he said. no other maid would ask me that. i'm studying philosophy. and economics.

o.

mary, he said, and he took a step towards me.

i took one back. what?

you always do this. as though i'm going to do something dreadful to you.

i seen what you do.

i am not planning to do anything to you. look, why don't you stay here, and make sure my father is all right. other wise he'll lock himself up in his study and draw birds and never eat.

i'll see what he wants me to do, i said. but i only come up here to help with your mother.

thank you. we appreciate what you did for her. what i said earlier. about my mother, you remember? when i said about her ill health. i regret it. of course she was more ill than i realized.

i shrugged.

i am trying to say sorry, he said.

there ain't no need to say sorry to me, i said. the person you wanna say sorry to is gone now so it's too late. see you got to think about things before you do them and say them.

he smiled. you don't change, do you?

no, i said. but maybe you ought to.

he shook his head and laughed. anyway, he said, thank you for what you did for her.

i shrugged again. and then i left the room and went down the stone corridor and up the stairs and then up the other stairs and i went in to my room.

edna wasn't up there and i was alone. i opened the window for some air and lay down on my bed and closed my eyes.

the autumn is a time when leaves come brown and curl and die. and you can not find the very first leaf which is turning. for summer and autumn move slowly in to one another. there is not one day when all the leaves are brown.

and the autumn is a time when i find the mushrooms under the leaves and moss and i take them home to cook and there is the one which if i split it open it bleeds and milk comes out.

and seven days after mrs was in the ground mr graham asked me to make up a tray of tea and so i laid it with a pot and a cup and saucer and strainer and a jug of milk. and i took it to his room and placed it on his desk.

sit down, mary.

i always know, i said, that you're gonna say summat when you ask me to sit down.

he smiled. then perhaps you should go and get yourself a cup and have one with me and make yourself comfortable.

i'm all right, sir.

but i would like it if you would go and get a cup and join me.

and so i did and went and brought it from the kitchen and put it on the tray and mr graham went to pour the tea and i tried to do it but he told me to sit.

i ain't used to someone pouring it for me, i said.

he passed me my cup. do you want anything else?

i'll have a puff on your pipe.

he laughed. i don't think so.

so what do you want to talk about? i asked. you ain't asked me here to sip tea and pass time in idle chat.

you are very sharp, aren't you? he said. i can't say intelligent for you are entirely uneducated, but you do bring something.

and what would that be?

i suppose a native cunning or wit.

is that different from an educated brain?

yes, i suppose it is. it's unformed, more animal, primitive.

animal?

i don't mean that as an insult. animals are survivors. they know what to do without having to be told. look, don't let it worry you.

there ain't a lot i let worry me. if i can't do nothing about summat then i don't let it worry me. if i can do summat about it then i put it right and then there's no need to worry anyway.

mr graham put his hands together, pressing finger tips on finger tips and making a steeple. you, he said, could teach the rest of the world a lot.

i laughed. i don't reckon i got nothing to teach no one.

you have. mary. i want to thank you.

you ain't got nothing to thank me for.

i have. for helping with my wife. she liked you.

good. but, sir, now she's gone, is my job over?

i would prefer it if you stayed here. i asked your father and he said he was perfectly happy with the arrangement.

but if you asked him and he knows you want me here and you'll pay him money, then he won't let me go home. that means you ain't left me with no choice.

but we need you here. mary?

i said nothing. i stood up and walked to the window. looked out at the grass which was covered in dead leaves and dew. the seed heads were drying out on the flower stems.

mary?

i turned to him. i don't have no choice, do i?

and so that is how i didn't go home like i always thought i would.

and that is how i came to stay.

and it was the next afternoon and mr graham was out seeing a woman what had a husband who died and edna was cooking and i was tidying the white room again. and i found a pile of books what was on the floor behind the table and i started to put them away with the others and i don't know what made me do it but as i was putting one of them away i held it. and the pages fell open. and i looked at them and turned them this way and that. but i knew nothing. no matter how hard i looked at it i could understand nothing of what it said.

mary?

i jumped and held the book close to me. i was looking so hard i didn't hear the door go and didn't hear him come in.

what are you doing? mr graham asked.

i ain't doing nothing, sir. i was on my way back to the kitchen.

let me see.

we stood there in the afternoon sunlight and he took the book off me. he held it in his hand and turned it over.

why did you take this one?

i shrugged.

go on.

the colour.

he smiled. as good a reason as any.

there's gold on it, i said.

as i said the words he moved the book and the sunlight glanced off the gold letters.

can you read any of it? he asked.

no. all looks a mess to me. don't understand how anyone can make nothing of it. just a lot of black lines.

not when you can read it. tell me, can any of your family read?

no.

no one ever tried to teach you?

i laughed. no. too much work to do.

i see. he pointed at the gold on the front of the book. see this, he said, see the letters. t. h. e. they make up the word *the*. you see? *the*.

and i looked down at the book and at the gold letters and he passed me it. and then he left the room and i stayed there and the book was in my hand and i was still there as the light left the room.

i told you i wrote this with my own hand.

i told you my sister beatrice would hold the bible and would read out. but she didn't know what the shapes were on the paper. and she could not read.

i told you.

and then next day the job i hated. i had to wax the banisters from the top floor down to the stone floor. i put on the wax and let it sink in to the wood and then rubbed till it shone and my arms ached.

mary. mary.

i could hear his voice from where i stood at the top of the stairs. i didn't do nothing but stayed doing what i was told.

i heard him go through the rooms then he come up the stairs.

ah, there you are, he said. what are you doing?

i think, i said, that with your educated brain you could see what it is i'm doing.

be careful you don't cross the line, he said, or you will become impudent.

can you be something, i asked, when you don't know what it is?

i think so, he said. the fox can be a fox without knowing it is one.

i'm not a fox.

i wasn't implying you were. look, i wonder if you would like to come with me.

you want me to stop this?

you can continue it later.

if that's what you want.

i do.

so i put the cloth and the wax on the floor and i followed him down the stairs and in to the study.

he pointed at the chair opposite his, on the other side of the table. and he told me to sit down.

and so i sat in my chair and he sat in his.

all right, he said. where to begin?

he took a sheet of paper and dipped his pen in the well. he wrote on the paper two lines. one along and the other coming down from the middle of it.

T

that is a t, he said, and it begins the word *the*.

he drew again on the paper.

t

this is also a t, he said. and that also begins the word *the*.

each letter has two ways of being. one upper case, one lower case. T. t.

i don't understand, i said.

you will.

i can't do it.

you can, mary. here. try and letter it out. draw it with your finger so you remember it. T. that's it.

as i drew with my finger on the desk he spoke.

a line across, he said. another line down. good, do it again.

and i did it three times.

that's it, he said. now try the other t. a line down with a curve at the bottom. a line across.

i traced it with my finger on the desk. a line down with a curve. a line across.

you see? he said.

i nodded.

i did see.

i did.

that night i went out after all the jobs were done. i walked up the lane towards the hill and the ground was damp and the long grass wetted my skirt. i stopped in the gateway and the field was full of the heifers and they were chewing and the noise was loud and the crows was calling and flying round above the trees and the moon was rising up and the stars was starting to show their selves.

i leaned on the gate and felt it with my fingers and the lichen covered the wood and i could smell the damp in the air and then my finger started to trace out the letter on the gate.

a line along. a line down.

T

*

and then although i took his shaving water in each day i noticed he stopped using it for the water was still clean and there were not small hairs floating in it. and his beard started to grow through and it was ginger and white like a fox tail.

and i took his tea in one morning and he was sat at his desk and he held his head in both hands.

i put the tray down but he didn't move.

are you all right, sir? i asked.

he dropped his hands and looked up at me. his eyes were watered and red.

can i get you summat?

no.

i didn't know what to do so i stood there.

mary, he said. take a seat.

i sat down on the chair by the door.

he looked over at the window where the wind blew the leaves up in to the air. and the leaves fell from the trees like rain.

pour the tea, will you?

so i did.

i sat and waited and he drank from the cup and it looked tiny in his hand. then he looked up at me. i didn't ask if you wanted a cup, he said.

i know.

i'm sorry. he half stood up.

i don't want one anyway, i said.

he nodded and sat back down. he looked out of the window again.

i've been so busy, he said, running around doing everything after the funeral. and it seems that it has come home to me that i am alone here now. and my son has gone as well. he turned to look at me. i'm sorry, he said. i don't know why i think it's appropriate to confide in you.

you ain't got no one else, i said, cos you're the one what everyone talks to.

he nodded. of course you're right.

it ain't the same without her, i said.

no.

we sat there a bit and he passed me his cup and i poured some more tea for him.

i've been out for a walk this morning, he said. i saw your father on the hill.

did you talk to him?

we stopped for a moment, he said.

shall i guess what you talked about? i asked. the harvest, the weather, what birds you'd seen, how good the apple crop was.

very good. but you missed one topic of conversation. he said he's got the thresher coming in this year. i didn't have him as a man of new technology.

he's a man of money making.

farmers usually are.

then he fell silent again.

am i done? i asked. can i go?

not quite yet, he said. he opened the drawer which was his side of the desk and lifted out a book. which was the letter we did? he asked.

i can't stay here now and do this, i said. i got jobs and edna'll clip me one if i shirk.

i will tell her i asked for you to be in here. now come on, which letter?

t

good. and do you remember how you draw it?

i ain't thick, sir, i said.

i am not insinuating that you are. i merely ask.

i remember everything.

good. then you will be my star pupil. right. this word. what does it say?

that one's a t.

good. now when it's next to this one, h, it becomes soft. th. th. *the*. so let us practise that.

and he showed me how to draw h, and then how to draw e.

and now, he said, we can put them together. we have t. h. e. and that makes up the word *the*. you see. *the*.

we drew the letters with our fingers. t. h. e.

good, he said. you know a word now. your first word.

so i can read a word?

you can, yes.

o.

and then he explained the letter b. b as in boat and bottle. only there was b and B. and i had to learn the both of them. and we wrote them with our fingers and then he made me write them with the pen what i dipped in the inkwell.

and then when we had done the letter what has a dot on the top and the one what is a straight line he said it was time to see how i could read.

and he took out a book and he said look. see if you can read this.

and the letters were in gold on the black leather and i looked at all of them and made them out and said each letter and then he made me join them in to words for that is what you do.

and there were two words and i knew there was two for he showed me how there is a space between words.

and i read the words.

the

bible

the bible, he said. well done. those are your first two words. now look at this.

and he took out three different books from his drawers and he showed me all of them was the same. *the bible*. and i read them all.

i read them.

my first two words.

i placed my finger on the letters on the small black book and made their shapes. and as i felt the letters what were carved down in to the leather i read them aloud. *the. bible*, i said. *the bible*.

he clapped his hands together. excellent. you are going to learn fast, he said. he pointed at the book what was in my hands. that, he said, is for you to take away and whenever you want you can look at it and remind yourself what you have learned.

this is mine?

indeed. you can keep it.

i held the black leather book in my hand. i held it tightly to me.

don't lose it.

if you think i'm gonna lose this then you're a soft bugger.

mary!

i'm sorry. i am sorry, sir. i didn't mean to say that. it come out cos i'm so passioned.

passionate, he said.

passionate, yes. i stood up. thank you, i said. thank you. i started to go out the room.

mary. the tray.

that night edna and i went up at the same time. the candle was on the box between us. she got in to bed and the bed sighed and i pulled my book out from under the covers.

don't blow out the flame, i said.

i tipped the book towards the light and looked at the gold letters on the front of it.

what you doing? she asked.

see this. this letter. the line across then down. that's a t. this word says *the*.

where you get that? you stole it?

no. he gave me it.

i opened the cover and looked at the first page, leaning in towards the candle to see. it was a mess of black lines and marks but i looked slowly along till i found another one. there. t. h. e. *the*.

i looked along the lines till i found three of them. *the the the*.

i closed the book and leaned over and blew out the candle. the smell of the taper was in the room. an owl called outside the window.

get some sleep, edna said.

and so i closed my eyes but my heart was beating fast with excitement and though my body stayed still in the bed my mind rushed around and would not stay still for it was like a bee in summer.

the next morning i went out with the peelings for the hens and harry was in the garden and he was raking the last leaves up in to the fire.

and i called out to him. morning.

and he stared at me but said nothing.

i tipped the peelings in and the hens rushed up and started messing around with them.

you finishing off? i asked. edna says you're done for a while.

harry nodded. all stopped growing, he said.

careful, i said. you just spoke.

he shook his head and turned away.

i pointed at the potatoes. shall i take them in?

he passed me the bucket. and then he gave me a bowl of the last raspberries.

nice day, i said. and i put one of the raspberries in my mouth.

is it?

i looked up at the sky. the sun is there, i said, only it's hid by a cloud.

you ever see the bad in life? he asked.

i'll have time to think about that, i said, when i'm dead.

he shook his head and turned away to walk over to the glass house.

harry, i said.

what? he turned back.

the raspberries are good.

got to grow less, he said. now there's only the vicar. gonna put some to grass.

that's a shame, i said. cos you keep it nice.

he nodded and almost smiled. then he walked off with his spade and went to clean up the glass house and put it away till spring.

i was in the kitchen when there was a knock on the window and i looked up and saw beatrice outside.

edna was up the stairs so i went to the door.

it's grandfather, beatrice said. mother said you'll wanna come.

so i told her to wait and i ran back inside and knocked on mr graham's door only there was no answer and so i found edna and i told her i was going to the farm. and before she could say nothing i ran back down the stairs and threw my apron down in the kitchen and went out to beatrice.

and we went fast as we could down the lane and to the farm.

we went straight through the yard and scullery and in to the kitchen. mother was there and she said you better go on in. and they stayed in the kitchen.

grandfather was in the apple room. and he was in his bed. he had a blanket over him and his face was turned away so he never saw me come in.

i ain't opening my eyes, beatrice, he said, nor eating nor nothing till she comes home.

i put my hand on his shoulder. i am home, i said.

he turned his head towards me. you are? well bugger me.

beatrice come and got me, i said.

i told her to, he said. been long enough and i ain't seen you.

but what's wrong with you?

nothing.

nothing? she said mother sent her up for me. said we'd be lucky if you lasted the week.

i know, he said. i told them that to get you here.

then the door opened and mother came in the room. how is he? she asked.

he ain't his self, i said. i'll sit with him a bit.

right then, mother said. i'll leave you to it.

the door closed and we both put our hands to our mouths not to laugh out loud.

i'm hungry, he said once we'd stopped.

i'll sneak out in a bit and get you summat. so how you been?

how've i been? a bloody misery. no one comes in and has a

laugh with me. your father's out all hours. he works those girls even harder now you ain't here. your mother's running round doing all sorts. and all that's made worse cos your father's been shouting that violet's having a baby. says she looks like a cow about to drop. how's she gonna have got herself in calf?

i spec like every other woman what's had a baby, i said.

now you're being forward, he said. so what's it like up there where you are now? you don't look much like you no more. you're above us now. you'll be speaking proper next.

don't be soft.

well. what's it like?

i spend all day polishing stuff which is only gonna get dull and need polishing again. got to wax all the wood and put tea cups and saucers on trays. got to wear a clean white apron every day.

waste of time. what's the matter with them all?

they ain't got nothing better to do, i said. they ain't got work from sun up to sun down.

don't spose.

but he gave me this, i said. i put my hand in to my pocket and pulled out my book and showed him.

you won't be needing no book, he said.

i pointed out the gold letters on the front. i can read this word, i said.

so you're gonna learn to read?

he's teaching me and i'm gonna do it.

what d'you wanna do that for?

cos i can. cos other people can.

grandfather laughed. you won't be needing words down here, he said. there ain't no books to read here. only teats to pull and horses to lead and eggs to gather.

and sheep to herd, i said.

and shit to shovel, he said.

and bollocks to castrate, i said.

now now, he said. can't have you speaking like that now you're growing to be a young lady.

i ain't ever gonna be no young lady.

so you gonna read to me then?

i only know two words.

he started to laugh and then i did too.

you better learn some more, he said, or you ain't reading to me. i'd soon get bored with two words over and over.

i am gonna learn more, i said. and when i have i'll come down and read to you. would you like that?

you'd make an old man proud.

then i'll do it.

you'd better hurry up. i ain't getting no younger.

don't say that.

it's true.

he tried to sit up and i helped him. he grabbed my hand. mary, he said. get me summat to eat.

you're sposed to be dying. what am i gonna say?

say i must be so pleased to see you i got the old appetite back.

i'll tell them i forced you to agree to eat.

that'll do it.

i stood to go.

mary.

what?

make us a cup of tea and all.

i stayed till it was near dark. i helped mother with the butter. and then i went out in the yard to go home and that is when i saw violet who was coming back from feeding the pig.

her belly was sticking out and the rest of her was thin as a wheat reed. and then there was the way she was walking same as one of the ducks in the yard. her hips moved like they was stuck to each other.

what you gonna do when it comes out? i asked.

she shrugged. dunno, she said. i told them i didn't know whose it is. i told them it was one of the casual hands.

did father believe you?

reckon he didn't have no choice. he said i can't keep it. says it's got to go.

you gonna let it go?

don't have no choice.

she looked down and kicked a stone with her foot. he ever say anything? she asked but she didn't look at me.

ralph? i asked.

yeh. him.

he's gone, i said. to university. i did tell him.

o.

we stood there for a moment.

he say anything about it?

not really.

o.

i got to go, i said. keep an eye on grandfather.

yeh.

and i left. and she stood there and when i turned round before the bend in the lane she was still standing there.

mr graham called me in his study again that night. the lamp was lit and the thick curtains drawn. the fire burned. i closed the door as he asked and sat at the desk.

did you bring your book? he asked.

i took it out my apron pocket and put it on the table. i

opened it and showed him the words i found. look, i said, i
know what this says.

good. and this word again?

bible.

excellent. now let us start on the first line. we have the
word *in*, then this one you know.

the.

exactly. *in the* . . .

i know that's a b.

good. b. e. g. i. n. n. i. n. g. that spells out *beginning*. *in the
beginning*.

that night i opened the book again by the light of the candle
and i read with my finger going slow beneath each letter. *in
the beginning*.

i traced with my finger upon my bed. i made all the letters
so they'd be fixed in my head for i didn't want them to go.

i blew out the flame and edna slept only i couldn't sleep
and i traced it again and again on the sheet.

in the beginning.

winter

this is my book and i am writing it by my own hand.

it is now the year of lord eighteen hundred and thirty one and i am still sitting by my window and i am still writing my book.

i can see my own face in the window glass. my hair and my skin is pale.

i am bent over and my pot of ink is in front of me and a pile of papers is to my left.

and you see how i had to learn every letter what i am now writing.

i don't like to tell you all this. there are things i do not want to say.

but i told my self i would tell you everything that happened. i said i would say it all and for this i must do it.

autumn changed in to winter so quickly i thought i had lost some days.

each morning in the dark of the room under the eaves, i pulled my clothing in to the bed and waited for that they were warm enough and then i put them on. the house was silent and i got up before edna was awake and before mr graham was downstairs. and i went in the study and cleaned out the ashes. i laid the fire new with wood and paper and lit it then went in to the kitchen and lit the fire there in the range then i had to go back to the study and keep an eye on the fire in there so it was warm enough for when he came down. and then i had to get the hot water for his shave before making the tea and preparing for the breakfast.

my hands became chapped and raw.

i did tell edna how cold it was and asked could she come down some days but she said i was used to getting up for the milking that we did every morning and for this i would be used to the cold.

yes, i said, but then i had the cow's heat to warm me.

the door in to the white room was kept closed and the door in to the dining room was kept closed so those rooms did not have to have fires and we put covers on the furniture. and we put stops by the doors so the drafts did not go in. we used only the kitchen and the study and i placed rugs down on the flagstones in the hallway.

mr graham ate all his meals in his study on his own.

it was dark when i got up and dark when i went to bed.

the kitchen was warm and edna did fall asleep by the fire in the afternoons and i sat on the wooden stool and peeled the vegetables.

and then one day mr graham went away to visit ralph and was gone for a week and we did some special cleaning where we scrubbed the whole house and waxed it again no matter how cold the rooms were and we went in to the church and we cleaned that and my hands was more sore.

and then the day come when mr graham returned.

the horse and carriage stopped outside and we rushed out to get his bags and edna made a big breakfast of bacon and kidneys though it was not really morning and i took it in to him in his study what was warm for that the fire was lit ready for him.

welcome home, sir, i said.

thank you.

how was ralph?

he smiled. he was well, thank you. he seems to be enjoying studying. i'm rather relieved as you can imagine. and how has it been here?

we done what you asked us to.

good. and the weather?

it was cold like this though the sun was out most days. reckon it was to show us where we missed with the cleaning.

how odd. we had no sun at all. in fact it rained every day.

he picked up his knife and fork and started to cut up the bacon. then he saw i hadn't gone. is there something else? he asked.

yes.

well go on, speak before my food gets cold.

i wondered, sir, will you have time to learn me some more?

teach. will i have time to *teach* you some more. i teach. you learn.

then can i learn some more?

he nodded and smiled. you are eager, he said. we'll continue this evening. we will start on writing tonight. yes. that's what we will do.

that afternoon i peeled the swede and cut off the end what was had by the frost and i got it ready for edna but she didn't come in the kitchen. i went in the garden and in the cold store in case she was getting some other vegetables but she wasn't there. i went up the stairs and up again and in to our room. and i found her sitting on the bed in the cold and she was holding her shawl around her and she had her box on the bed. i asked her if she was all right.

i'm going, she said.

and i asked what did she mean? where was she going?

i'm leaving.

why?

mr graham said he didn't need me no more. he said now mrs graham is gone and ralph has left there ain't enough for two of us to do.

there is.

he said he'll get someone in to help with the heavy clean but that he couldn't pay money for the two of us. and he give me this.

she showed me the money he'd given her then she stood up and held her shawl tight around her. i knew when you came, she said, that he liked you more than he liked me.

ain't that, i said.

it is that. but it's all right. it ain't your fault.

and then she was gone and the room was empty and i sat

there till the light was going and i had to go down to attend to the fires and make sure there was enough heat to cook on.

and so i cooked and i kept the fire burning and then when the evening came i took a tray of food in to the study. and he was sitting in his chair and he saw me come in.

ah, mary, he said, and he stood up. i think there's no need to bring my food in here. i'll come in to the kitchen and eat with you. it's warm in there and it'll save you carrying trays around.

and so i carried the tray back to the kitchen and he followed me. and he sat down at the scrubbed table opposite me and he started to eat. it took him a while to look up and realize i wasn't eating nothing.

what is it? he asked.

edna's said you told her to go.

he put down his knife and fork. ah, he said. so that is what has put you out of sorts.

she weren't happy.

i know. but it is easily explained as it was a simple matter of mathematics. i can't afford to have too many staff when there is only me in the house. we can get outside help in when necessary.

but she was here a long time, sir.

i know.

she'd been here longer than me. she wanted to be here.

are you saying you do not?

that, i said, ain't what i'm saying. it was edna's home.

he put his hands together and smiled. you can not possibly expect me to be responsible for her all her life.

can i not?

no.

and he picked up his knife and fork and started to eat again but i did not.

eat, he said. please.

and so i pushed my food around my plate but did not eat it. he finished his plate full and i took the two plates through to the scullery. and he watched me.

i realize, he said when i come back, that it must seem unfair.

i said nothing.

look, will you sit down? you haven't eaten anything.

i'm not hungry.

you need to eat. he shook his head and stood up. well, he said, we have things to do. in fact, wait there.

he left the room and i stood there.

i heard his study door open and then soon after it closed and i heard his footsteps returning down the stone corridor and he came back in. he was carrying the pen and inkpot. he also had some papers and the blotter.

it seems a shame, he said, to move now we're here in the warm. he went to pick up the rest of the plates from the table and i stopped him.

that is my job, sir.

i took them through to the scullery and wiped the table with a wet cloth and then a dry cloth and he put the papers down.

here, he said, pointing to the chair beside him. sit down.

and i did.

where is your book?

i put my hand in to the pocket of my apron and brought out my black leather bible. i put it on the table.

open it.

i did.

read.

the room was silent and the flames of the candles burned and at first it looked as though the small black marks were moving on the page. and so i put my finger under the words and as they stayed still and i started to say them i could feel him leaning towards me and it seemed like he wasn't breathing. it seemed like he was willing me to read each word.

that night i lay in my room upon my own bed and the other bed was empty.

the air was so cold i could see each breath as it passed out of my mouth. and even though the cold hurt my face and arms and hands and i was shaking with it, i sat in bed with the book and i read by the light of the flame.

in the beginning.

i have to stop for a while.

i have to shake out my hands and walk about the room.

i have to look out of the window and rest my mind from thinking on all this.

at times to have a memory is a good thing for it is the story of your life and without it there would be nothing. but at other times your memory will keep things you would rather never know again and no matter how hard you try to get them out of your head they come back.

i will continue but in a moment.

the next day i woke early and it was still cold in the house for the cold was in the walls. but it was raining outside and the frost was gone. i went down the stairs to light the fires. i boiled the water and made tea and got it ready to take in to the study only when mr graham got up he came straight in to the kitchen.

are you all right? i asked for his skin looked thin and white as the paper in my book.

i feel a little under the weather, he said, and he sat down heavy in the chair.

can i get you anything? i asked.

no.

i lit the fire in your study so you can shave in there.

i'm fine in here, he said.

you want me to pour the tea? i asked.

no. i'll do it, he said.

do you want anything to eat?

no. thank you. i just need to be quiet.

then i'll leave you alone, i said. i poured the flour in to the bowl and added the yeast and salt and some tepid water what i had warmed on the fire and started to work the dough.

he sat for a while then poured the tea and drank half of the cup. he watched me for a while then he stood up. i'll be back later, he said.

are you seeing one of your old ladies? i asked.

but he never answered. he went out the room quick.

and he left.

i pulled the dough off of each of my fingers and covered the bowl and rested it by the fire to rise. then i made some pastry and got a hare that had been hanging for a few days and i skinned it and cut it up and cooked it in a gravy all morning.

later i went outside and pulled three leeks and they come out easy where the frost was gone. and then i got some potatoes in from the cold store. i stood out the back and saw the light was going and there was still no sign of him.

i boiled the potatoes and leeks and i put the plates to warm for they was cold from the scullery and then i heard the back door open. and he came in to the kitchen.

is it ready? he asked.

few minutes, i said. are you all right?

he clapped his hands together and rubbed them. yes, i'm fine thank you. he sniffed at the air. it smells good, he said. i think we'll eat in here again this evening.

and so we sat down. but before i put a fork of food in to my mouth he put his hand out to stop me.

we shall say grace, he said.

he closed his eyes and clasped his hands together and he said for what we were about to receive, we should be truly grateful.

i listened to him and thought about the day i'd had and the cooking and the standing in the rain pulling leeks.

why, i asked, do we have to be grateful to god when it was me what went out and picked the food and me what cooked the food?

mary, he said. and he put his hand up to stop me but i carried on.

and it'll be me, i said, what cleans up after the food.

he laughed. you are nothing but a heathen.

he ate all i gave him then asked for more and ate that. and then he pushed away his plate.

is the fire lit in my study? he asked.

yes. i lit it earlier for i thought you'd be back.

good. will you bring the tea through?

and he went. and so i took the plates out to the scullery first and then boiled the water and got the tray ready. pot, strainer, cup and saucer, jug of milk. the small spoon. all proper. all as i had been taught.

i carried it along and the door was closed. i placed the tray down and opened the door then picked it up again. i took it in and put it down on the desk.

close the door, he said.

i closed it.

sit down, he said.

i sat down.

we're going to have a lesson now.

now? i said. i ain't finished clearing up.

you can do that later. come on, where's your book?

so i got out my book and lay it on the desk in front of me.

where were we? he asked.

you were doing the next few words, i said.

ah yes, so i was. he cleared his throat. come, he said. bring your chair around here. it's impossible to work like this, where one of us is seeing the text upside down.

and so i picked up the chair and carried it to the other side of the desk and sat by him.

that's better, he said. now look at the shape. you need to remember it is like a snake. ssssss. start with the pen at the top.

i dipped the pen in the ink and i started at the top and the line curved and there it was. s.

and that is when i felt his leg press against mine and i moved away for there was not enough room behind the desk with the two chairs. only his leg followed and continued to press against mine.

come on, he said. do another. do a whole line of them until your hand will not forget how to do it.

and then i felt his hand drop to my knee.

as i write these words i find i can not breathe and i reach for the window and i try to open it to let the air in but i can not and so i lay my head upon my hands and upon my papers.

i allow my self the comfort of a short dark sleep.
but then i wake and i must continue.

i did not know what was happening or why. and i said to my self do not jump to your feet and start saying anything for this could be just a touch between two people. and if i said anything i would look stupid.

but then his hand started to go up and down upon my leg and i am deeply shamed to say that i did not move.

i did not know what to do.

he said, what is the next letter? he said, concentrate and tell me what this says. and i did not move.

and i told him what the next letter was and the next and then he said i should write them down for to remember them.

and so i did.

and as i did, his hand moved on my thigh and the pen was dipped in the ink and then scratched upon the paper. and i lay down the pen when i had done the letters and i said, now i must go for i have so many jobs, and i jumped up out of my chair.

and i moved the chair back the other side of the desk and i picked up the tray and he said, no. leave it.

so i left it.

i left his study and i closed the door.

that night i could not sleep. i could not close my eyes.

the next morning i was tired and did not want to get out of bed for the cold but also for the reason that i did not want to go downstairs. but i got up and went down in to the kitchen and started the fire and i put the water on. and i went out in to the hallway and i was about to go and clear out the fire in the study and lay the new one, when he came down the stairs earlier than is normal. i did not look up at him but i kept my head down and hurried back in to the kitchen.

and yet he followed.

the water is not hot, i said, and the fire is not laid.

that is all right.

you wait in here, i said, and i'll go and do it.

and i rushed out to do the fire and i did kneel down and scrape out the ashes and then i laid it with kindling and i did light it and wait till the flames was caught and i put some logs on and then i went down to the kitchen and told him it was lit. and he went in his study.

i boiled water and took it to him and i did his tea and before he could come and eat in the kitchen i took him in his break-fast and closed the door quickly.

and then i busied my self and i was glad that with edna gone there were all her jobs and mine. though there were only two of us the fires burned as many logs and the floor got as dirty.

that day he went out to the church and to visit some people and i made a stew with the turnips and some carrots and put it with the hare what was left and that evening we ate together in the kitchen. and when he finished he said i had to go in his study for we were to have another lesson.

can we have the lesson in here? i asked.

he shook his head. no. all the books are in there.

please. it's warmer in here.

he stood up. you have to come in to my room, he said, other wise there will be no lesson and then as a result you will not learn to read or write, and i know you want to.

*

i know what you think.

don't go, you think. don't go in to that room.

but i did.

i boiled the kettle and made up the tray. i stood watching the leaves spread their colour in to the water.

i put the lid on the pot. i put the jug on the tray. i put the cup on the tray.

i picked up the tray.

and i took it to his room.

and i closed the door behind me, like he said. and i saw the chair was by his chair round that side. and i went and sat in the chair next to his. and i waited while he opened my book.

ah yes, he said, this is where we are. now i want you to read this whole sentence then you can attempt to copy it out.

and then he brought out an old ledger.

this is yours for writing in, he said. it will be kept in here and you can do all your practising in it. if you continue like this you will soon be able to read and write. you are such a quick learner. you really are doing exceptionally well. right. let's make a start, mary.

and so i ran my forefinger along under and slowly made the letters in to words and then he showed me how if there is a small dot it divides the words in to sentences. and i said them aloud.

and all the time his hand was upon my leg.

and then i was done with the reading of them aloud and it was time for me to copy it out in to the book. he pushed the inkwell towards me and i dipped the pen in to the ink and let the excess ink fall down in to the well. and i touched the pen on to the paper and i slowly made the letters and the letters made the words. and while i did it he put his other arm about my shoulder. as though it was a shawl warming me.

the fire shifted in the grate and a log fell down. i went to rise up to check for any sparks of embers but he pressed me back down in to my seat.

it'll settle, he said. now continue.

and so i did.

and he stood up and he put another log on and he sat back down and his arm creeped about me again.

and then when i finished writing out the letters, he said, look, see how you did. see how good you are at this. and then he put his hand under my chin and turned me to him and he put his lips to mine and the smell was of tobacco and tea and his moustache was unkind and he opened his mouth and i felt his tongue creep in to my mouth.

i must stop for a moment. breathe.

and he closed my black leather book and he took my hand in both of his.

i know this is wrong, he said, but i have been so lonely.

he did not look at me. i did not look at him. i did not know what to do so i went to close the ledger and tried to stand up.

no, he said. you must blot it first for the ink will stain the other page.

he showed me how to put the blotter to the page to soak up the ink which gathered in pools at the end of the letters.

and then he took the ledger from my hand. i tried to take it back but he would not let me.

it is mine, i said. you gave it to me.

but it must stay in here, he said, for this is where you will have your lessons.

and if i do not come in for my lessons?

then, he said, you will not learn to read and write.

we sat for a moment in silence. there was only the sound of the flames and the sound of the lamp. the wooden walls and our breathing.

you understand?

i nodded. yes, i said.

he smiled. good, he said. it is good to have a shared understanding.

that night i lay in my bed with my whole body stiff and though i swore to stay awake until the sun was with us again i was so tired for the lack of sleep the night before that i fell backwards in to stillness.

and the first i knew of anything was the feel of something in the bed.

in my sleep i thought it was edna getting in to her bed and it was the feather mattress sighing but then i felt skin touch mine. and i knew it was someone in my bed. and then i thought it was beatrice and she was in the bed with me but it was not.

and then i heard his voice as he was praying and asking for forgiveness and i felt his arm about me.

and he lay next to me and that is all. the two of us in the bed.

i tell the truth.

if i was not telling you the truth why would i have told you any of it?

i did sleep for a while but it was sleep where you do not lose yourself and then i woke and felt him in the bed with me and i could hear his deep slow breathing and though it was cold i did not put my clothes in the bed to warm them. i got out of bed and dressed and without looking at him i quickly left the room.

downstairs i laid the fires and lit them. and then i boiled the water.

and when he came down he was dressed and ready for the day and he looked right at me only i did not look back.

i will take my tea and breakfast in the kitchen today, he said.

and so that is what he did.

he had breakfast and then he went to his study and he locked himself in for he was writing the sermon for the next day in the church and i knew not to disturb him for he always said he needed time to think. and so i did my jobs and did the cooking and got in the vegetables and washed them and peeled them and cut them. and then later i heard the door go where he went out and i stood by the open door and heard him tell harry not to disturb him when he come up for the horse and the garden for he had a lot of writing to do. then he went off visiting and i heard the door again when he came in after dark. and later he came in the kitchen and we ate together. and after we carried the lamp in to the study where i had lit the fire and we sat on the two chairs.

and he leaned forward and he did that to me again where his tongue tastes of tobacco and feels in my mouth like a calf's liver.

and then he opened my book and he said, now where were we?

and i showed him and then he opened the ledger and he helped me read what i had written the day before and then he taught me a new letter i had not seen before. and i read some letters and then i wrote them.

and yes his hand was on my leg. and yes his arm was around my shoulder.

and yes he did slip his hand with its cold skin underneath my bodice.

when i was done and i knew all the letters that were in the book i left him in there and i went up to my room. i got in to bed with all my clothes on and i blew out my candle. i stayed still.

i heard one creak on the stairs then it stopped. my heart felt like it would stop too. and then i heard another step. and another. i heard the door handle being turned. the door opened and closed. i heard the floorboard creak in the room. and then i felt the weight on the bed and through my eye lids i could see the light. i opened my eyes. there was a candle in the room and he was undressing and his skin was white and i closed my eyes.

he lifted up the cover and moved me towards the wall and he got in beside me.

he put his arm around me and put his tongue inside my mouth and he stroked me and then he reached down to my legs.

stop.

there is a reason for me to tell you all this.

you will understand.

he reached up and put his hand under my skirt and i pushed him away but he did it again and then he pulled one of my legs away from the other and he pushed his hand in between the legs.

and his fingers slid inside.

i tried to speak only he said shhh and then he reached over and he blew out the candle.

and then he climbed upon me and his knee forced open my legs and he was on me and he forced himself in to me.

and it did hurt.

but i did not cry out.

and he was sweating and his breathing was heavy. but then he rolled off me and was soon asleep.

i did not sleep.

and when the morning came i pushed the bedding back to get out of bed and i saw the blood and i saw my skirt was covered in blood and i took it in to the kitchen and i burned it upon the fire.

and from that day on that is how we lived. every morning i got out of bed first and i went down the stairs. i lit the fires and when it was warm he come down and had his breakfast in the kitchen. on sundays he went to church and he asked me that i stayed at home and made his dinner. other days people would come to see him or he would go and see them. and saturdays he would write in his study with the door closed and some days he went walking or he watched birds from his window and then he did drawings and wrote some notes saying what the birds were doing.

and harry would come one time each week and tidy the garden and dig the soil and check the glass house. and he would come each day to the stable only he knew not to come to the house.

and if i had a quiet moment i would sit at the kitchen table and i would look at my black book and see what it is i learned.

and then each evening we sat together and ate in the kit-chen.

and then each evening we went in to his study and i dipped the pen in the ink and wrote words.

and then each night he followed me up the stairs and in to my bed. and his knee went between my legs until i started to open my legs for then there would not be bruises in the morning.

and all those weeks i learned more letters until i knew all twenty six. and i could write them and i was starting to know more words and they were starting to match with the words which were in my head.

the weeks went by and it was a hard winter and the frost was on the inside of the windows so for this i could not see out until the fires was lit.

and in the bedroom i was only there in the dark and though there was frost i could not see out anyway. and so i pinned a thick blanket over the glass and i put an extra blanket on the bed.

and one morning i started to get out of the bed and he pulled me back in and in the warmth of the bed i fell to sleep once more. and when i woke it was light and i was cold and i saw he had pulled the covers off me and was looking at me.

i got out of the bed as quick as i could and pulled on my clothes and ran down the stairs.

and as i was lighting the fire in the kitchen there was a knock on the back door and when i got there it was hope and she was smiling and she told me violet's baby was born.

she told me how they spent a night waiting and when he was born he cried.

and she told me they buried the cord under the ash tree for him to have a good life.

and she told me he was a boy.

and his hair was the colour of mine.

and his hair was the colour of milk.

and when hope left and i went back in to the house i thought of them at the farm and how the baby would cry in the night and if i was there i would wake to him and hold him and i should be in that house and not in this house with people who were not my family. i wanted to go down to see him but i could not for i had too many jobs to do and so i got my head down and got my work done.

and it was not many days till i stood outside in the lane and watched them come to the church. mother carried the baby in her arms. beatrice and hope and violet followed. and they let me hold him in his shawl and his fingers held around mine and he opened his eyes and he looked at me.

we went in to the church and mr graham blessed him and put water on his head. and after we all passed him from arms to arms. and then mother took him. come on, she said, come to your mother.

i looked at violet. she didn't look at me.

and then they said they had to go back for the milking and i had to stand outside the church and watch them walk all the way back down the lane till i couldn't see them no more.

i walked slowly back in to the house. mr graham was sat in the kitchen in the chair by the fire and he was reading a book.

he looked up when i came in. have they gone?

yes.

it's wonderful that you have a brother at last, he said. your father must be thrilled.

i said nothing but got my head down again and got the flour and yeast out to make the bread. and then he told me

he got a letter and ralph had written to say he was coming
home for a night for it was christmas coming the day after.

and so i cleaned his bedroom and aired it and waxed the
wood on his bed and made it ready for him. i made the bread
and a cake and it was all ready.

and mr graham was busy for being in the church and having to see more people.

and that night we had the lesson and i read out to him.
then he come after me. up each of the stairs. he undressed by
the light of the candle and got in to the bed with me. he held
me in his arms and then i opened my legs but that is not what
he wanted.

for he started to cry. and for the first time since he had
come to my room at night we spoke.

why are you crying? i asked.

i feel such guilt.

then don't come up here. if you feel guilt it is because it is
wrong so do not do it.

but it has made me happy.

so it makes you happy *and* guilty?

yes.

and you can not have one without the other?

no.

then do not come up. for then you will not feel guilt.

but i want to be happy. o mary, he said. let us not talk in
circles all night.

the truth, i said, is you do not want to be honest about
what it is you do.

i did not wake until late the next day and so i had to rush
around lighting fires and heating up water. i made the breakfast and started boiling the ham. and then i heard the carriage

stop outside and i heard a voice then a knock and a shout as the back door opened and ralph came in to the kitchen.

mary, he said, his voice alive. did you miss me?

no, i said, my voice dead.

i know you did. and father wrote to tell me that you are in sole charge of the two of us tonight.

i am.

then let us see how your cooking is.

is that why you came back? to check on my cooking?

he laughed. of course not.

he watched me for a while, then asked how my family was.

if i had a day off from here, i said, then i would be able to go and see them but i do not for your father prefers only me to look after it all.

i know. he wrote and told me.

but there is some news, i said. and as i said it i watched his face very carefully. violet has had a baby son. though they are saying it was my mother who had the baby.

o.

and i think he looks very like you, i said.

all babies look the same, he said.

they do not.

they have round heads and two eyes and a mouth.

but the eyes and mouth are very telling, i said.

you have seen him, then?

yes. because he is a boy my father is letting him stay.

so he will be brought up on the farm?

you sound disappointed, i said. don't you want him to be?

no.

so if he is nothing to do with you why do you care?

mary. you do not change. no sooner than i walk in here you have me in a trap. you like to set your snares.

and that is when his father walked in the room.

ralph, he said, and the two men shook hands. how was your journey?

it passed soon enough. i am here now.

and you have to leave the day after tomorrow? mr graham asked.

ralph turned to look at me. i'm no sooner arrived than he is asking when i leave. you wish to get rid of me, father?

don't be silly. i wish you to stay. that is why i ask how long you can be here.

then let us go in to your study and catch up, ralph said. mary, bring us some tea.

and so i did. i carried it in to the room where they sat together and the chairs were one on either side of the desk. i put more wood on the fire and then left them.

i lit a fire in the dining room and opened the curtains and removed the covers from the table and chairs and they ate their ham in there. and then that afternoon they walked together and at night they ate in the dining room again and then had tea in the study which meant that i had to keep all the fires burning.

and then they went to church for midnight and the bells rang loud. and i did go as well but i had to hurry back in the cold for to stoke the fires in their bedrooms. and then i returned to the kitchen and damped the fire and took my candle and went up the stairs to bed.

and i was alone and i slept well.

and the next morning i got up early for there were too many jobs for one person to do and i lit all the fires and heated the water and started to prepare the big dinner and then ralph came in the kitchen and sat by the fire. he watched me prepare the tea tray and cook the kidneys.

my father tells me you are a very good student, he said.

does he?

he says he has taught you the whole alphabet and that you are starting to be able to read some words.

yes, i said.

it's quite an achievement for a farm girl.

is it?

of course it is. mary?

what?

are you all right? you're much quieter than you used to be.

i'm fine, i said.

something's changed.

no. nothing has, i said, and then i left the kitchen and went in to the scullery so that he could not watch me or ask me any more questions.

and he helped me by keeping the fires burning in the dining room and study and i served the dinner in the dining room and i went in to the kitchen and i sat and ate on my own by the fire.

and i did think of mrs. and i remembered how her hand rested up on my head and she stroked my hair.

and then they was back to the church while i was clearing it all away and i washed the plates and glasses and pans and i swept the floor and i did find the last of the turkey feathers in the scullery where i plucked it.

and the next day ralph came to see me and to say goodbye, and said he would see me next time he came home. while i'm not here, he said, look after the old man for me. see he has everything he needs for he lives more and more like a pauper with not enough help.

and then he left.

*

and it was back to the two of us.

and then it was the time when the year turned in to the next year and eighteen hundred and thirty became eighteen hundred and thirty one by the years of our lord.

and that is the year it is now while i am writing this.

and soon it was the sixth day of the new year and time for the blessing of the ploughs. and so we both went to the church in the morning and i watched as father came up the lane with the horse and plough and they unhitched it and pushed it in to the church along with the other ploughs in the village. and i followed in and sat in one of the pews and i could see father and mother and violet and beatrice and hope. and mother held the baby.

and when they went we stayed in the church and mr graham told me to open the big bible at any page.

so i did.

he told me to read what page it had opened upon.

i ran my finger along the words and i did sound them out one letter at a time and then when they started to come they got faster and i was speaking the words aloud and i was reading. i raised my voice louder and then i found i was reading faster and i did not have to always put my finger there.

and then i imagined writing the same words and i knew my hand could do it and make the shapes of the letters.

mary.

what?

the words you read just then, he said. the bible is telling you that you must open your heart and give.

but i have no more to give, i said to him. for i have given of everything i had.

i turned and left the church and walked back to the house.

*

i went through the back door and down the stone corridor and i opened the door in to the white room and went in and i closed it behind me. and i looked around at the covers on the chairs and table. and i pulled back the blue curtains and looked out at the bare trees and the frost on the grass where it was still white. for though the sun was out it did not touch the grass under the trees.

it was cold in the room and the cold went through my skin.

and then i turned towards the wall and looked at the books. and i thought about when i first went in the room and how i hadn't never seen a room like it.

i walked over to the books and i took one out. i held it in my hand and looked at the cover and then i carefully opened it and there were pages with tissue in to protect the drawings but i looked at the words and then i found i could work them out and i turned page after page to make sure but i could read it even though i was slow. where had been a mess of black lines there was now letters. and words. and sentences.

and then i closed the book.

and that is when i knew i was done.

i could read and i could write.

i was done.

that afternoon he followed me in to the kitchen and stood and watched while i worked. only there was a knock at the back door. when i went to answer he left the kitchen and went along to his study for he did not want to be caught talking to his maid. and it was mother standing there. she held a cheese which she handed to me.

it's for him, she said. tell him he still owes for the last one.

i took it off her and put it in the scullery.

you all right? i asked. the baby looks well.

got a good appetite.

how's grandfather?

still alive.

tell him i'm trying to come and see him. there's just too much to do.

i better get back, she said. he's waiting out there.

and she went.

and the door closed.

and i went in to the scullery and cut the new cheese with the wire and thought about when mother said the person to taste the new cheese would have a baby. and i was careful not to taste it but i cut down through the cheese and cut it again in to smaller pieces, then i curled up the wire and put it in my pocket. i put some cheese on a plate and cut up the new bread and got a new jar of chutney down from the shelf.

i put it all ready to eat and placed a net upon it and i stoked the fire and then i sat by the fire for a moment. only i couldn't stand to be in the house so i went out. i walked out of the garden and i went to the churchyard and i sat on one of the graves and i thought of them down at the farm and me up here. i thought of the baby there. and grandfather and mother and my sisters. and how if i didn't get back i would forget it all. and then i thought of how i had read aloud and did not even have to run my finger beneath the words.

and i did not mean for to be out so long but i could not make my self go back. and then he come out the house and i could hear him calling my name.

and then he found me.

i thought you were never going to come back, he said.

i said nothing.

it's freezing out here, he said. going to be quite a frost tonight. come on in.

and he tried to take my arm but i pulled away from him and then i walked to the house and he followed.

i went in to the kitchen and went to put wood on the fire.

i've already done it, he said. i thought you would need the fire lit in order to cook for us tonight.

i said nothing again but i walked past him and went to the scullery and took the net off the bread and cheese and chutney and took it to him.

o, he said. is there not a hot meal?

i said nothing. i left it there and went out the room and up the stairs. i took off my dress and my apron and i put back on the dress i wore the day i came from the farm. it hadn't been washed and i held it to my nose for that i could smell the farm on it. i put my apron back on top.

i sat on my bed for a while until the light had gone from the room and i had to feel my way down the stairs. he was still at the kitchen table and the candles were lit.

mary, he said. come on, this isn't like you.

i put on a kettle of water to clean the dishes.

will you not talk to me? he asked. i demand that you talk to me.

and then i turned to him. you demand? i asked.

i demand, yes.

you may pay for me, i said, and you make me stay here but you can not demand me to do everything you like.

i know i sound like i was being calm but i was not. my heart was beating so fast it felt like it would leave me. my hands shook and i tipped over a glass but caught it before it smashed on the flagstones.

mary, he said. you're usually so cheerful. such a positive presence.

i know, i said. that's what your wife liked, ain't it? that's why she wanted me here.

why are you being like this? we have been happy, he said.

no, i said. you have been happy.

he pushed away his plate. will you talk to me?

no, i said, i'm done with talking and i'm tired.

you still work for me, he said.

i stared him in the eye. i did notice, i said.

i took the plates through to the scullery and washed them up. when i went back in the kitchen he was still there at the table.

will you make tea?

yes, i said.

bring it to my study. and put an extra cup on the tray.

he left the room and i heard his footsteps go down the corridor and i heard the study door open and close.

and i did make him his tea. i poured the water on the leaves and they unfurled in the pot.

but i did not put an extra cup on the tray.

i took the tea to his room and placed it on the desk.

and as i turned to go he said, mary. stop. i have prepared a lesson.

no, sir, i said, for i must go and finish my work.

but the work is for me and i am your employer and i have asked you to stop.

i shook my head. i don't think you understand, i said. i can read and write as much as i need now, sir.

you still have so much to learn.

but i know enough for what i want to do.

which is what?

i don't know yet, i said, but i will one day.

you know you can not leave here, he said. if that is what you are thinking.

you do not know what i am thinking, i said. now excuse me, for i have work to finish.

and i left.

i went and finished my jobs then took the candle and went up the stairs, up again and in to my room. the cold was in the walls and the mattress. as though each feather in the bed was frozen hard. each floorboard coated in ice.

i got in to my bed in my clothes and lay there, curled tight until some of the heat from my body had gone in to the bed.

and after a while i began to thaw and i blew out the candle and lay there.

it was not long before i heard the feet on the stairs. i heard a few steps climbed then it went silent, then a few more steps.

i knew who it was.

i knew what it meant.

the handle turned slowly and i got out of bed and i tried to close the door in his face, but he forced it open and pushed me back against the wall. and he came in the room and closed the door and put his candle on the box. and he pushed me on to the bed. and he climbed upon me so that i could not move.

what's happened? he asked. have i been cruel to you? i have treated you well, haven't i? i have looked after you.

i don't want you to be in here any more, i said.

you never complained before.

he pushed a hand under my skirt and tried to put it between my legs but i kept them closed. he tried to stick his tongue in my mouth and i kept it closed.

don't make me do this, mary, he said. and he pushed my

legs apart and put his knee upon my bad leg so i could not move. i felt the cold air on me.

please don't, i said. please.

but he grabbed my wrists and held them and he forced my legs open further with his knee and he pulled down his clothes and he pushed it inside me.

and it did hurt.

and when he was done and he was sweating and his breathing was slowing he held me in his arms. i'm sorry, he said. i didn't want to hurt you. you mustn't fight then it won't hurt. you understand?

i said nothing. i lay there. i remained still. i remained rigid.

let us go back to how it was, he said. we'll do a lesson tomorrow night and then we can come up to bed and i promise not to hurt you.

he didn't wait for me to speak but he fell on to his back and in to sleep.

i lay there for a while. then i pulled down my skirt and covered my self for i was sore. and i pulled down my apron.

and it was then.

not before. then.

i felt in my apron pocket something. i put in my hand and pulled out the cheese wire.

i did not think. what happened next i did not think or plan. and that is the truth as my god is my witness.

i gripped the two wooden ends of the cheese wire and i held it up to his neck and i did not think about what i was doing but i pressed down as hard as i could and he started to make a noise and it was dark and i did not know what i was doing and i pressed down like i did on the cheeses and i held it there and his arms and legs started to try and fight me off but i pressed harder with all my weight and then there was a terrible sound and i felt the heat of the fresh blood rush upon my hands.

it was hot. and it smelled.

and there was a lot of noise.

he stopped moving and the hot blood slowed and i let go of the wire. i jumped back off the bed.

i ran to the door and felt for the handle. i opened it and went out. i felt my way down the stairs, placing my hands on the walls and banisters, and then i was on the landing and i went down the next stairs to the bottom. i went along the stone corridor and i went in to the kitchen. the embers in the fire were still warm and i put some kindling on and waited for it to take. and when the flames burst out i put on some small logs.

now you will think i am not being truthful but i am when i tell you this. my hands were not shaking and my heart was beating so slow i thought it might stop. i was like i was moving in my sleep.

the logs caught light and the flames rose and i pulled the chair to the fire and i sat there.

it is hard to say what it is that happened in my mind that night as i sat in the kitchen. i watched the flames move and i put fresh wood on when it had burned down. and i watched the window to see when the sky was going to get light.

i was sore between my legs and my hands hurt but i did not like to think why it was that my hands hurt.

i did not like to think. and my head was empty for i made my self think only of the fire and the light and the cold.

and then the window got lighter and it was dawn and the light filled the room and i did not put any more wood on to burn.

and i stood up from the chair. i looked down at my self and i could see where the blood was all over my arms and my apron and my skirt. i took them off and threw them in to the fire and watched them burn. i went in to the scullery and i washed my hands in the white enamel bucket and the water turned pink.

and then i went down the stone corridor to the bottom of the stairs. and there on the white walls were the red hand-prints where i had felt my way down.

and i climbed up the stairs and there were more handprints. and they got more red as i went up to the landing and then more red again as i went up to the top floor. then i stood in the doorway of my room. i kept my eyes down and could see where the blood had soaked in to the floorboards. and i could see his arm which hung from the bed and touched the floor.

and i was cold and i put on my other skirt and apron and i pulled on my boots and i had to step close to the bed for to get the book which he had given me and which was on the box and i put it in my pocket and i didn't mean to but my eyes looked up and i saw him lying there and the wire was still in his neck.

and then i did start to shake.

i walked right up the hill and i sat upon the top of it for a long time. the ground was cold and i wanted it to hurt me where i sat.

i could see where i wanted to go.

i looked down at my hands and the line around my nails was red with blood.

and i stood up and i started down the hill. as i got down i didn't walk along the lane but along the edge of each field, close to the hedge, for i did not want to be seen. and as i got near the farm i creeped along until i reached the small shed behind the barn and i went inside.

there was some old hay and i made a bed from it and i curled up in it and i did not eat or drink and i did not sleep but i stayed there and i tried to empty my mind so that i did not think and did not remember what happened.

later when the light went from the sky and i was under the cover of the dark, i got up and went out in to the yard. i drew some water from the well and found some stale bread in the bucket what was waiting for the pig. i dipped the bread in to the water and ate it. i went back in to the shed.

i did sleep that night and then in the morning i was woken by voices and i heard the cows when they came in for milking. and then i heard the baby cry and i wanted to go to him but i did not dare.

and so i stayed there all day but then before it got dark i heard some new voices. it sounded like two men and they were talking with violet and then with mother and father. and i heard them say the gardener had found him. and then they did say they was gonna look around the farm. i piled some hay over me and i lay still. i could hear them calling to each other and then i heard a voice come near to the shed and i lay still but the door opened. and then i heard someone come right up to me and move the hay which was hiding me and then i could see that it was father and he looked at me and i at him. and behind him i could see a man in the doorway and father covered me up again.

no nothing here, he said.

and they left.

later when the two voices had gone he came back and he uncovered me. i crawled out and brushed the hay off me.

you better come in, he said.

and so that is how i walked through the mud and shit of the yard and in to the kitchen.

mother was at the table and she turned to look at me but she didn't say nothing.

they'll be back, father said. so you ain't got long then you got to go.

i ran up the stairs and in to my old room where there was no bed just a dark rectangle on the floorboards where the bed had been. i looked round and saw the blanket still over the window. i pulled it to the side and looked out over the home field, at the shape of the hedges. and then i saw the cow lying down and she moved her head like as if she could feel me looking at her. and then i went in to the next door room and saw the two beds and beatrice's bible on her bed.

and then i went back down and in to the apple room only there was no one there, just the air thick with smell. so i went in to the other room and he was there on his chair, his feet propped on the other chair.

he looked at me for a long time. they're looking for you, he said.

i know, i said.

you better sit down.

and so i pulled up the chair and sat with him. i come for a reason, i said. and i put my hand in to my apron pocket and pulled out the black bible mr graham had given me. i opened it at page one and i started to read. *in the beginning*, i started. and i carried on reading.

he said nothing but sat and listened and watched me. i put the book down in my lap.

was that you doing that? he asked.

it was, i said. and i learned to write too.

but you ain't gonna need to do reading nor writing where you're gonna be going. they come here for you.

i know.

and they'll come again.

they won't have to, i said.

why?

cos i'll go to them.

i closed the book and put it in my pocket.

did i make you proud? i asked.

he said nothing.

tell me i made you proud.

he looked at me for a while, then said, when you was reading that, you made me proud. yes, he said. you did.

i nodded.

i got to go now, i said.

i know.

i stood up then touched his hand with mine and his skin was dry and cold. i squeezed his hand once more and then i left the room.

mother watched me walk through the kitchen and she was holding the baby in her arms and i looked at him then held out my arms. but she wouldn't pass him to me.

what you done?

i shook my head. i don't know.

where you going now? she asked.

back to the house, i said.

i went out through the door. my sisters stood outside in the yard and as i stood there in the dying light and wet mud i thought of the evening i'd last been there with the clearing of the barn. and the summer air. and all of us working. and the birds swooping in and the red sun and the sweet air.

   and then i walked out of the yard, past the three of them and past father, and i walked up the lane and i did not look back and i walked until i was back at the big house.

spring

this is my book and i have been writing it by my own hand.
every word i spelled out.
every letter i wrote.

i said i would tell you the truth of everything that happened and i have told you and it is all true except for one thing.

i said i was sat at the window writing this and i looked out and i could see the trees and the birds. i said i could see the rain run down the glass.

i said i could not see the fields for the weight of the mist.

i said i could see my own pale face in the window.

i said i could not breathe and i reached for the window to open it.

when i said all those things i was not telling you the truth.

for you see, i have no window in here. i can see nothing.

i have a wall in front of me. i have a chair and a small table and i have a bed.

i have some paper and ink and a pen. and i have a pot to piss in.

i have a door which is unlocked when i am given food and when they give me water to drink and wash in and when i am to empty my pot.

i can not see out. but the world is still there inside my own head.

when they first put me in here i did ask them for a pen and ink. and for paper. and for something to blot my ink with. and then i dipped my pen in to my ink. and i started to write.

my name is mary. m. a. r. y.

my hair is the colour of milk.

i decided to begin at the beginning and end at the end.

and i know what the end is for they will be coming for me soon and they will take me away.

i did have to write fast for i do not have long left. and i wanted to tell you what happened for you to see why i did what i did; it was not unprovoked.

but there is one thing more i wish to tell.

as the sun rises each day my belly swells.

as i have been writing this i have been sick.

i know i am with a child.

if i tell them they will leave me in here with the door locked for the rest of my life, and they will take the baby from me and i will never see it again.

i will not let them do that.

and so i tell them nothing.

and they can take me away.

i know what they will do to me. they will put rope about my neck, as i put the wire about his. and i will hang until i am no longer alive and my legs will sway above the crowd.

and my baby will die with me. inside me.

and my baby will always be with me and its hair may be the colour of milk but it will never be stained with blood.

and now i am done and there is no more to tell you.

and so i shall finish this very last sentence and i will blot my words where the ink gathers in the pools at the end of each letter.

and then i shall be free.